the MOSES BOTTLE

Russell Mead

A RAVEN HOUSE MYSTERY FROM

W🌐RLDWIDE

TORONTO · LONDON · NEW YORK

In memory of Dr. Joseph N. Kelly, who lived and practiced in our present home for many years. He wasn't Dr. Casey, but he put me in search of him. . . .

Raven House edition published September 1981

Second printing September 1981

ISBN 0-373-63003-4

Prologue

THE SKY WAS ANGRY, streaked toward sunrise with bruising shades of purple, mulberry and charcoal that, slashing down to the pale Atlantic, invited later storm. At the foot of the cliff the September beach was newborn, the sand a glistening nude beige where it met the water, for it was low tide. No people yet, no footprints.

Labor Day. The day when Cape Cod ended a chapter then began an entirely new book for those who lived on this peninsula all year round. Later, traffic would snarl across the two bridges that crossed the Cape Cod Canal, that were the links with the rest of the world. Dr. Casey wished briefly that he were leaving, too, then recognized the wish for what it was: a possible key to an escape route.

He was parked atop the cliff staring seaward; he had noted the colors of the sky and they matched his mood. He *was* angry, but it was an odd kind of anger. It would be more accurate, he supposed, to call it resentment.

Last night his profession had caught up with him in a particularly unpleasant way. He had gone to a party as an invited guest, and midway through it had become involved as a doctor, which was not in itself unusual. But his role as the area medical examiner had also been brought into play, and this, especially in a small town, made things difficult.

A man was dead. The circumstances were suspicious.

Dr. Casey scowled now at the North Atlantic, which was deceptively benign, considering the sky. He hadn't considered the dead man a friend; in fact, he had barely been an acquaintance. Looking back, it seemed as if the only times they ever met were at cocktail parties, smiling banal smiles, with glasses in their hands, mouthing empty words.

True, they were of two different worlds. Probably they never could have had a real meeting of the minds, and he contemplated this with a slight feeling of ruefulness, for he liked to think that he could relate to most people, even though, obviously, it no longer mattered in this case.

What *did* matter was determining what had caused this death—and what *kind* of a death it really was.

Admittedly there was a problem in waiting for the final pathological verdict, because such reports took too long even in the best of circumstances. In the interim, trails could be covered, clues could be altered, emotions could become sufficiently subdued so that personal camouflage became easier and easier.

This was the time to act, no doubt of it, but he didn't relish the thought.

He didn't relish it at all.

Casey shook himself, both mentally and physically, and faced a first decision, which was whether to drive home and try to get some sleep before the day really began, or to go across town to Jessie's Kitchen for breakfast.

Since there was little chance of actually achieving any sleep, he opted for the breakfast.

As he drove away from the ocean and down tree-shaded streets still slumbering before the tourist exodus, he told himself bitterly that he should have known better.

He had always detested cocktail parties. He should have said no to this one right in the beginning. . . .

1

THERE IS A TIDE to physical ailments, a certain rhythm to the incidence of miscellaneous viruses and other varying afflictions.

Early in his Cape Cod practice Dr. Casey labeled the end of summer "ear time." From late August through mid-September he inevitably peered through his scope into dozens of inflamed ears, most of them belonging to wriggling youngsters, and asked the same question: "Been swimming in the ponds?" The answer, almost always, was in the affirmative.

It wasn't that there was anything *wrong* with the fresh-water ponds. It was simply that sopping ear canals gave bacteria an open invitation when fresh water was involved. It didn't happen with salt water; this is a simple fact of nature. Kids were the greatest offenders because they tended to wallow in the water for hours on end.

The Friday before Labor Day there were ears and ears, and the lollipop tree in his waiting room had nearly been stripped. Shortly after 6:00 P.M. Dr. Casey locked his office door after his last patient left, just as the phone started ringing.

He was in no mood for an emergency, and he

even thought of letting his answering service take over, but conscience triumphed and he picked up the receiver.

"Lon?" The voice at the other end of the line was light, and all too familiar.

"Yes."

"Through for the day?" she asked, and he winced. She knew too much about his hours, his habits, and when the lady was a beautiful alcoholic that could become awkward.

"Not quite," he said cautiously.

"Oh? Swamped?"

"Ears," he said, which was true enough.

"Brats," she said, and laughed, but it was a mirthless laugh and incurred a certain wariness in him.

She said, "I won't keep you. It's about Sunday."

"Sunday?"

Carla Banning giggled, and this wasn't very funny, either. She said, "We're having a bash. Greg's people, mainly. They'll be going home Monday, most of them. But since we're going to be year-rounders now we want to have some of our local friends, too. You *will* come, won't you, Lon? You know people don't get sick on Sundays!"

He said carefully, "Carla, I'm not much for that sort of thing."

"Nonsense," she told him. "You've got to stop being a hermit. All work and no play . . . ."

"I know." He was trying to keep it casual, trying not to let his annoyance surface. "But I *do* play, Carla. It's just that my idea of play—"

"I know," she said. "Big slimy fish."

He laughed despite himself. He said, "Come on, now!"

"Anyway," said Carla, "there's Clare."

"What about Clare?"

"Well, I think she's been sleeping with Greg, though that's beside the point, really. You know my husband. He'll sleep with anyone paintable, but even so....."

Casey hesitated, not wanting to get into this area at all. He said, very carefully, "Don't let your imagination make trouble for you, Carla."

She was amused. "I didn't realize you considered me imaginative, doctor." He sensed her shrug. "I don't know," she admitted, "maybe I have a big-sister complex about Clare, but she's deep in her shell. Just like you. Come to think of it, it seems to me she's brightened up the few times you've been over here."

"That *is* pure imagination."

The light and lovely voice became a bit huskier. She said, "I hope so, because I rather want you for myself."

He said sharply, "I hope no one else is listening to this."

"Not a soul, love," she assured him. "Greg and Clare took sketch pads and went walking down the beach at least an hour ago. Make what you want out of that. And my faithful Mrs. Murphy finished the ironing and took off in her old beach wagon just before I called you, so I am alone. Completely alone. Also, I am wearing something filmy and seductive. How does that strike you?"

"Carla," he said. "Please."

"I'm in love with you, doctor," she told him.

"Look," he said, trying to get the conversation back on an even keel, "you're much too smart to go that tired patient-falling-in-love-with-her-doctor route. You, a famous model—"

"Ex-model."

He ignored that. "Married to one of our country's leading artists," he continued.

She snorted. "In whose opinion?"

In Greg's, certainly, Casey wanted to say, but denied himself the pleasure. And Carla said, "Oh, damn it all. They're coming back. I can see them from the window. They just started up the steps from the beach."

Thank you, Clare Evans and Gregory Banning, Casey said to himself. And, to Carla, "Where are you, in your bedroom?"

"Ah," she teased, "so you *are* trying to build up a mental picture. No, I'm in the living room. You can see all the way across the world from here."

This was close to fact. The Bannings lived in the section of town known as The Heights, topping great swooping sand dunes. Most of the homes in the area were rambling old wooden summer houses that had been modernized and converted for year-round living. Their owners possessed incredible views with tax bills to match, and a surprising degree of comfort and privacy. It was an ideal place to live except when storms came slashing in from the sea. Then life on The Heights could become an entirely different affair, with the electric power out for hours, sometimes, and the wind orchestrating its own wild symphony, shaking houses to their foundations, seemingly, and rattling windows for added sound effects.

Now Carla said irritably, "They both walk too damned fast. If you keep on arguing with me they'll be here before I've got you to commit yourself."

"To commit myself?"

"The party, darling," she said, being over-sweet about it. "Five-ish?"

He knew that he would later detest himself for having given in so easily. But, despite the fact that in his opinion Carla was on the verge of ruining both her body and her brain, she was sharp. An excuse would have to be a valid one and he was momentarily at a loss.

So he said, "Okay," then added, *knowing* that he should know better, "Carla . . . make the next one a cup of bracing tea, will you?"

Her laugh was light, mocking. "Lon," she chided him. "Your caduceus is showing!"

CASEY EMPTIED THE ASHTRAYS, plumped up the pillows, and restacked the well-used magazines. Looking around he told himself, as he had many times before, that he should do something to brighten up the waiting room, to say nothing of his own office.

The same was true of the house, he decided rather gloomily as he walked through the con-necting breezeway. He had added the breezeway

and the small office building after moving to the
Cape five years previously, and fortunately the
local builder he had chosen had a good head for
compatible architecture, so the result was pleas-
ing. Even Aunt Agatha, he told himself, would
have approved, but even as he thought this he
quickly converted "would" to "might."

The house had been a sacred trust to Agatha,
having been the Franklin homestead for well over
a century. Casey promised himself that when
things slowed down he would get out Agatha's old
genealogical records and go through them. He
knew there was some vague relationship to Ben-
jamin Franklin, but this particular branch of the
family had left the Boston environs and come to
Cape Cod way, way back.

Agatha Franklin definitely had been old New
England; D.A.R., Colonial Dame, an officer in
the Devon Historical Society. She was the last of
her branch of the Franklins, she had outlived
everyone else, and it seemed to him that in the
process she also had managed to accumulate
everything anyone else in the family ever could
have possessed.

Casey knew very little about antiques, yet he
realized that he owned a hoard of them. His
neighbor, Eleanor Chase, who lived down Fuller
Road toward Uncle Joseph's River, long since
had sounded the warning, "Don't sell anything,
don't give anything away, without consulting me
first," and her husband, Paul, had chuckled in-
dulgently.

"Be sure she doesn't wangle it all away from

you," he had cautioned, while Eleanor bristled with pretended indignation.

Eleanor wrote magazine articles about antiques, and when he found time to clear things out, Casey did intend to consult her. In the meantime, it no longer seemed as strange to be living in a dusty, potential museum as it had when he first came to the Cape, although museum or not, it hadn't mattered then where or how he lived.

It was only now that he was beginning to realize, fully, how little *anything* had mattered then. The Franklin house was there, it was his, it was a refuge. It had become a kind of personal cocoon.

Now . . . well, time dimmed the memory of tragedy; the pain became dulled at the edges. You found that you wanted to live again, and that could be dangerous, too, Dr. Casey told himself, as he went out into his old-fashioned kitchen, put a kettle on the stove and got out a china cup and a tea bag. He was about to follow the prescription he had given Carla Banning.

Maybe, he thought, poking around for crackers and cheese to go with the tea, that was the trouble with Clare Evans, Carla's sister. Maybe she, too, was now feeling loneliness where before there had been only emptiness. Maybe she, too, was beginning to want to live again, and with a man like Gregory Banning, proximity could be a hazard.

Clare was young, and although not as outrageously beautiful as Carla, she was lovely in her own right. Her husband had been killed in a plane crash more than a year ago. Early this past summer she had come to the Cape to visit Carla and she was still here.

Clare, like Banning, was an artist. In fact, if Casey remembered correctly, she had been a student of Banning's and had introduced Carla to him several years ago, so maybe that was all there was to it. Maybe it was purely a student-teacher relationship, even father-daughter relationship. Banning must be nearly twenty years older than Clare.

Casey, as he poured boiling water over his tea bag, found himself hoping that it wasn't any more than that, for he sensed a certain vulnerability about Clare. It was as if she stood ready to be hurt. Loneliness, following emptiness. Yes, it was dangerous, no doubt of it.

Philosopher, philosopher, he chided himself as he sat down at the kitchen table with his tea, some cheese, and crackers that had seen crisper days.

The telephone rang and he groaned. But this time it was Eleanor Chase.

She said, "Lon, people in New England normally have baked beans and brown bread on Saturday, but we're adding codfish cakes and having it all tonight. Care to join us?"

He cared.

2

Saturday was a good day. Office hours were from 9:00 a.m. until noon, when Dr. Casey locked the door, and turned the phone over to John Haynie's answering service.

He then went fishing with a friend who, amazingly, knew treasure holes yet undiscovered. They came back with a good catch of flounder, and when Casey insisted that he didn't want his share, since he had no intention of cooking the fish himself, he received a dinner invitation, which he promptly accepted. This led to two pleasant evenings in a row.

Sunday, from the beginning, was *not* a good day.

At five in the morning old Mr. Doane called to say that his wife, Clarissa, who was eighty, was having difficulty breathing.

There were times, at least in Casey's book, when house calls, even though usually undesirable, were indicated, and this was one of them.

As a result of his examination he put in a call for the town ambulance and followed it in his own car to the Cape Cod Hospital in Hyannis, this twenty miles up the Cape from Devon.

The hospital boasted a competent coronary-care unit into which Clarissa Doane was placed, after which there was the drive home and the thought of snoozing for a while since it *was* Sunday morning.

This thought was dismissed quickly due to a car accident with two "personal injuries" on Scallop Shell Road. Both victims were brought to Dr. Casey's office. They were businessmen from Boston, come down to the Cape for the Labor Day weekend. They had set out to do some early-morning fishing and had skidded en route to the beach. Neither was hurt seriously, but one did require several stitches to close a forehead gash.

This task completed, Casey brewed coffee, read the morning paper, then called the hospital to check on Clarissa Doane, who was doing surprisingly well. The call completed, he considered the idea of going over to Snow's Beach and taking a swim, then indulging in a hearty late breakfast, but this was not to be, either.

Ed Landers called up to report—apologetically, since it was Sunday—that his asthma was acting up, and since Ed *did* have problems it became obligatory to suggest that he stop by the office.

As Ed was about to leave the phone rang, and this time it was the police station calling to say that a summer visitor had just brought in a child with a badly cut foot. Would Dr. Casey take a look at it? Since there was evidently no other member of the local medical profession willing to do so on this particular Sunday, he agreed that he would.

And so the day went.

Breakfast, except for the coffee, was over-looked; lunch was a hastily snatched sandwich. The middle of the afternoon he *did* close shop, this with considerable resolution, and drove over to Snow's Beach. The tide was halfway out, so conditions were not ideal, but he wandered away from the main beach area toward a small inlet that snaked through the marshes, where the water was always deep.

For half an hour or so he swam, and emerged invigorated. Then, for a time, he lay on the beach, pleasantly anonymous with his head, face down, on a striped terry towel.

He wished very much that he had not told Carla Banning he would go to her party. He favored gatherings with compatible people who had something to exchange with each other and this, he knew from experience, was not the way Carla set about making up a guest list.

There would almost certainly be artists and writers and actors at Carla's party, most of them with extrovert tendencies that would make him feel like a tongue-tied clod. Possibly there would be a few locals or, more likely, people who had moved to the Cape from other places and brought their money with them, but he doubted there would be many *real* Cape Codders. They seldom came within the circle of newcomers like Carla and Greg Banning.

He, true, was not a Cape Codder. He had been born the other side of Boston, and to be a real Cape Codder one had to start life right *on* this peninsula almost surrounded by water. Nevertheless, the local town fathers had virtually given him citizenship last year when, to his surprise, the selectmen voted him Man-of-the-Year for his service to the community, and presented him with a testimonial at the annual town meeting.

He could not remember when anything had touched him quite so much. The testimonial now hung in his office and was oddly comforting. At times when his morale needed bolstering it gave the needed assurance that he had done the right thing in moving to Devon and putting out his shingle.

The legacy from his elderly aunt had come at a most propitious moment. He was finishing his residency at a Boston hospital, and the plan was that he would start practice in one of the more affluent suburbs the following fall. This had been his wife, Marcia's, idea. It had never been what he really wanted, for he had a certain missionary zeal when it came to the practice of medicine, which was not apt to be fulfilled in places such as Wellesley or Chestnut Hill. But he had felt he owed this much to her.

Had it not been for Marcia, he probably never would have become a doctor, and he was deeply aware of this.

They had met and married while still in college. She was a mathematical wizard, and later it was her job in one of the Boston area's electronic enterprises that put him through medical school.

For this he was overwhelmingly grateful to

her. She freed him financially so that he could concentrate totally on his studies, and he intended to spend the rest of his life repaying his debt to her. But it was not to be that way.

In the last summer of his residency, Marcia, working late one night to complete an important project, drove home in a blinding rainstorm, skidded on the wet road, and crashed into a tree. She died in the ambulance on the way to the hospital. His hospital.

They called him to the emergency room, where the doctor on duty was a former classmate of his. The shock was so tremendous that, for quite a long time, there was only numbness.

Later grief came in terrible, frustrating waves. He could remember only all the things he had never told her, and now never could.

He still flinched from exploring this time too deeply. It was as if the remembered bleakness was a chasm, and when he thought too much about it he still felt as if he were standing on a crumbling edge.

At the worst point of all, he had received the word of his Aunt Agatha's death and his inheritance.

One afternoon he drove down to look at the impossible old house in Devon, and he wondered what it would be like to stay and practice here, and decided to find out.

It took little investigation to determine that Devon needed another doctor, and his relationship to Agatha Franklin gave him immediate entrée.

From the beginning he was accepted into the social life of the town by all the various factions that existed within it, and there were a good many. An eligible man, he soon discovered, was always in demand. Devon hostesses, like women everywhere, inevitably had female friends who either never had married or were widowed or divorced.

He was not quite thirty when he came to Devon, and he soon came to realize that young doctors were considered especially good catches. But this amused, rather than bothered him. He still was not interested in husband-seeking females, although he had stopped mourning Marcia. There was that chasm still, but there was no longer that acute ache for what should have been between them and never had been.

He supposed he had learned acceptance, which was a dreary word, used in this sense. He had even achieved a certain measure of contentment here in Devon with his friends, his practice. Where women were concerned he had trod carefully because it was a small town and obviously difficult for him to maintain a low profile in it.

He recognized desire for what it was, and knew that it could easily tempt him toward women like Carla Banning, and this was something he simply could not afford, especially in Carla's case.

He remembered the first summer she came into his office with one of her periodic sore throats, and how familiar she looked. This, he later realized, was because many of the commercials she had made in her modeling days were still being shown on television.

She had given up her career to marry Gregory Banning, and from what Casey had heard, few of their friends would have given odds on the marriage lasting as long as it had. Greg Banning was nearly old enough to be Carla's father, but it wasn't that that mattered so much; many September-May marriages worked out beautifully. It was, rather, the simple fact that Greg Banning was a total bastard.

Having mentally delivered this opinion, Casey rolled over on his side and looked directly into the eyes of an elderly woman in a pink bathing suit who was sitting under a beach umbrella.

"Why, doctor," she purred immediately, "I didn't realize it was you."

"Good afternoon," he said pleasantly, stood, and gathered up his beach towel and sandals, making his exit with a friendly wave before she could start telling him about the ache in her right hip.

3

THE BANNING RESIDENCE made a perfect party setting. It had been the summer home of the Peter Chilson family for many years, the Chilsons having owned one of Boston's major department stores. With the elder Chilson's death, the estate had been divided among a number of squabbling heirs, and this segment finally sold to Gregory Banning.

Dr. Casey drove past the house and parked his car down Heights Road so that if he needed to make a hasty exit he could do so.

He walked back slowly, and was nearly at the Banning's sandy driveway when a bright blue Land Rover pulled up beside him, with Tony Mayo at the wheel.

"Where did you park?" Mayo asked him.

Casey pointed. "I have to be able to get out," he said.

"So do I," said Mayo, "Wait for me, will you?"

Casey was more than willing to wait. Also he knew that the need to be able to exit quickly in the event of an emergency was as important to Tony Mayo as it was to him. Mayo was the reluctant owner of the Parkington Funeral Home. His grandfather on his mother's side had established the business, his father had married into it and Tony had become the inevitable heir.

He was, at first encounter, an unlikely undertaker, although Casey saw no reason why undertakers should, of necessity, be pale and unctuous and black-clothed. Tony, though, was a bird of exceptionally bright plumage; clothes were not exactly an obsession with him, but he was closer to sartorial splendor than any other man in Devon. He was tall, he was dark, he was handsome, and as he strode back up Heights Road today he wore a burnt-orange jacket, milk-chocolate slacks, a pale beige shirt and a tie in which orange, beige and chocolate were blended with touches of gold. The tie did not shout, to be sure, but neither was it subdued.

Casey could not possibly have put together the component parts to achieve Tony's kind of effect; his own blue tweed-blend jacket and dark blue slacks needed a professional pressing job, and his blue shirt and striped tie were definitely dull. However . . .

Tony said, "It's a hell of a day for a cocktail party."

They turned up the driveway. The gray-shingled bulk of the Banning house loomed just ahead of them. Since it was a faultless afternoon insofar as the weather was concerned, with the ocean a proper shade of sapphire and the sky suitably decorated with marshmallow clouds, Casey raised an eyebrow and Tony Mayo said, "We should be fishing."

"Amen," Casey agreed.

They walked around to the front of the house, both knowing from past experience that Carla's parties tended to spill out onto the lawn that overlooked the ocean and—this usually later—on down the long, rickety flight of wooden steps that led to the beach below.

People fluttering like noisy, oversized butterflies hovered principally in the area of the bar, which had been set up on the terrace at the edge of the lawn. It was being presided over personally by Barton Smith, of Smith's Services, who wore a blue, gold-buttoned jacket that looked as if it had been unearthed from some ancient attic trunk.

Carla appeared, swooped, kissed both Casey and Tony Mayo then stood back and said, "Dear God—the two handsomest men in Devon arriving at the same time!"

Tony beamed, but Casey winced. Carla, obviously, had already got a good grip on the situation through alcohol. She was not riding high as yet but she was heading upward, and she looked disconcertingly beautiful in the process.

She was tall, model-slim, with the even-featured face that had made her so tremendously photogenic, widely spaced gray eyes, and light. ash-blond hair of the shade, Casey remembered, Marcia used to call expensive. And Carla was expensive; every inch of her was expensive. Fortunately, Banning evidently could afford it.

She led them to the bar. She watched with a proprietory interest while Barton Smith made a vodka screwdriver for Tony and poured Jack Daniels on the rocks for Casey.

She said, "Greg's showing someone through his studio. A male, would you believe? But he's rich, and he has his wife in tow."

She smiled impishly at Casey, willing him to respond, but although it took willpower the smile he returned managed to be primarily fatherly. This was the stand he had elected to take with her, although there was probably not more than four or five years difference in their ages.

She said, "Oh, there's Brent Nickerson," and Casey grinned despite himself.

"Now *there*," he said, "*is* the handsomest man in Devon."

Nickerson was vice-president of a local bank and most of the year he preserved a perfect banker's image, but briefly, each spring, he shone during the annual production of The Scallopers, a surprisingly good amateur theatrical group that put on a once-a-year benefit performance of leading Broadway musicals.

Nickerson's voice was close to professional in quality, and when it soared through the auditorium at the old high school where The Scallopers's productions were held, he was romance incarnate.

Carla said now, "Beauty, male or female, is in the eye of the beholder, Lon." Then she flounced away to greet her new guest.

Tony Mayo eyed Casey narrowly. "She has one going for you," he said.

Casey shook his head. "She only thinks she does."

Mayo laughed. "I wouldn't be so sure. Oh, God, there's Florence Page."

It was Casey's turn to laugh. "She has one going for you?"

"Let's hope she only thinks she does," Mayo countered.

Florence Page was an artist with a summer place on The Heights and a New York studio. She had made a name for herself in the field of wallpaper design, also offering coordinated draperies and personal decorative advice to those few who could afford it.

Her technique was to center her planning around a painting after a study of her prospective clients' personalities. From the painting, colors were chosen and then the wallpapers and fabrics evolved.

Dr. Casey could remember an evening when Greg Banning had called Florence a prostituted hack right to her face. Thus he was faintly surprised at her coming to the party.

She had been talking to Clare Evans but upon seeing Tony Mayo she smiled and waved, then beckoned, and the two men made their way across the lawn to her.

Florence bestowed dazzling smiles on both of them, but her gaze lingered on Tony just as Carla's had on Casey. She was a tall, thin woman, dark skinned, dark haired, a Gypsy sort of person who, while not pretty, was striking.

Clare Evans, on the other hand, was very pretty. She was shorter than her sister, Carla, with a pleasantly rounded figure, lovely copper-colored hair, and astonishing blue eyes almost the color of the wild chicory that grew along the roadsides.

She said quietly, "Hello, doctor."

He said, "Hello," and took a steadying gulp of whiskey.

Florence said, "Labor Day," which was probably an adjunct of something else she had been saying that he had missed, and Casey picked it up, hoping he was on the right track.

"You don't have to go back to New York yet, do you?" he asked.

"I may," she said. "Perhaps I can get back for a few weekends before I close the house but, would you believe, it looks as if I'll be working with Greg Banning's guests. How about *that*?"

"The Van Houdens," Clare said, by way of explanation.

"*The* Van Houdens," Florence elaborated. "They are Hudson River people; they're like the Roosevelts. They have one of those vast estates on the river and they've just bought a penthouse in the East Sixties and they're interested in redoing both. Wonderful, isn't it? It should let me have my winters in the sun for years to come. If I can win out, that is."

"Win out?" Tony Mayo asked her.

"Just now, Greg's showing them through his studio, and I rather imagine he's making the pitch of the century."

"But," Tony said, feeling his way in this foreign field, "he doesn't do, well, wallpaper, and the other things you do."

"He could always find someone else who does," Florence Page said practically. "His thought would be to do the paintings. A painting for each room, around which everything else could be coordinated. He *does* have the name. Nevertheless. . . ."

Tony said, "I thought that Banning despised the idea of anything commercial."

"Darling," said Florence, with a light but nasty laugh, "why do you think he's been doing magazine covers these past few years? He can *say* it's for wider exposure and all that rot, but *I* say it's for one thing only. Money. When you get right down to it, that's what most people work for, isn't it? Except you, perhaps, doctor. But then doctors don't have to be money motivated, it just comes to them. Even you, Tony. . . ."

"Oh, come *on*, Florence," Tony protested.

She laughed and said, "I need another drink."

They started for the bar and Casey, left alone with Clare, at once felt tongue-tied. She was wearing a simple white dress with a single ornament: a large gold medallion emblazoned with a lion.

He said, indicating it, "That's unusual."

"My Zodiac sign," she said. "Leo. My husband gave it to me."

So, thought Casey, strike me out again.

He knew very little about Clare's marriage, principally what Carla had told him. He knew Harrison Evans had been a public-relations executive in New York, and Carla had done some modeling through his agency. She had introduced him to Clare, just as Clare had introduced her to Gregory Banning.

When Evans had crashed in his private plane, he had been killed instantly. The crash, if Casey remembered correctly, had been somewhere in the Poconos, and Evans had been alone at the time.

Then, this past summer, Clare had come to visit the Bannings and he had met her for the first time. Their few subsequent encounters had been on those occasions when Carla invited people in for drinks, or a barbecue, or to go swimming.

This, he was quite sure, was the first time he ever had actually been alone with Clare, and even now they were standing on the edge of a crowd. So he didn't know her well enough to feel, as he was feeling, that there was something wrong. Whereas Carla was inclined to overdo her makeup, Clare applied hers with a light touch, but it was applied skillfully.

Even so, there were shadows under her eyes, a tautness to her lips, a certain anxiety, almost a *fright*, evident especially when her face was in repose.

Now she smiled slightly and said, "Have you reached a diagnosis, doctor?"

He flushed and said, almost stammering, "I'm sorry."

"Well," she said, only slightly reproving, "you *were* staring."

He fumbled. He asked, then was horrified at his own bluntness, "Is something the matter?"

You stupid fool, he told himself. Carla has already said that she suspects Clare has been sleeping with Greg. If Clare is in love with Banning, that in itself would be trouble enough, wouldn't it? And what possible business of yours is it? What business, indeed!

Yet, surprisingly, there was only one way he could describe the reaction his question evoked in her. Caution. Although her composure didn't falter for a minute he would have sworn that she gripped her glass just a little bit tighter, and her very blue eyes seemed to become veiled.

Caution. Why should she be *cautious*?

Clare said lightly, but with a bite to the words, "Does something seem to be the matter, doctor? Or do you simply make it a practice to go around searching for symptoms?"

It would have been kinder, he thought, simply to have slapped him.

4

GREGORY BANNING HAD BUILT a gray shingled studio at the far side of the house, which had weathered sufficiently so that it seemed a natural part of the whole complex. Now a white-haired man emerged from it, followed by a plump, silver-haired woman, followed by Greg, who was wearing what Carla called his artist's uniform; faded jeans, leather thongs, and a white shirt open at the throat with the strange-looking copper disk he claimed he had found near the ruins of an old temple in Mexico, hanging from a black silken cord around his neck.

Banning was arrestingly tall; six-feet-four at the least, perhaps an inch or so more. To Dr. Casey's professional eye he looked like a man who had had too much; too much liquor, too much drug experimentation, too many women—though Casey was cynical enough to suspect that it was a while since this last had been a real problem.

Nevertheless, time had given him a certain "ravished" look that seemed to be singularly appealing. Women of all ages fawned over Gregory

Banning, and he encouraged them, at least to a point.

He stopped at the bar, and Casey saw Barton Smith reach down to some secret place, his hand emerging with a green bottle with an unusual shape. Banning nodded approvingly and the bartender poured a drink and handed it to him.

The Van Houdens had moved on across the lawn and were chatting with Carla. Clare, who still stood at Casey's side, her verbal thrust unanswered, said, "I think they're leaving. That'll upset Greg's apple cart."

Casey realized, with a start, that there was definite dislike in her voice when she spoke of her brother-in-law.

He asked dryly, "Why should it?"

The lovely blue eyes *were* shadowed, no mistake about it. Clare Evans was tired, she was worried. She answered him almost absently. She said, "Florence Page wasn't entirely sure of her ground, but she's right. Greg *does* want a commission from the Van Houdens. He wants a contract that will mean doing a painting for each room in their new penthouse, plus the old Hudson River mansion they plan to restore. Then he'll have friends take over when it comes to coordinating colors and draperies and rugs and all the rest. He's even asked me to get in on the act."

"Will you?"

"No," she said, with surprising directness. "I have no desire to work for Greg. He's just as commercial as Florence thinks he is, though he'd go

to any lengths to protect his sainthood in the eyes
of the public.''

Ouch, Casey thought. You've been burned—
but how? Is it personal, or because you wish your
sister had never married him, or because you
worshipped at his altar when you were an art
student and there is nothing more disastrous
than unveiling an old clay-footed idol?

He said, ''Banning really *is* setting up a
business enterprise, then?''

The blue eyes swept his face briefly. She said,
''Banning would *like* to set up a business
enterprise. Banning needs like *hell* to set up a
business enterprise. Banning is *broke*!'' Then, annoyed at herself, she asked, ''Why am I telling
you this?''

She looked up at him, and he had the disconcerting feeling that for the first time she was seeing him as a person, that until now he had merely
been one of Carla's friends, somewhere in the
background, maybe just Carla's summer doctor,
not even so much as a friend.

He wondered how he did seem to her. Middle-
aged, probably. She was younger than Carla, but
he was not all that old, damn it! Nevertheless,
he'd been feeling a bit paunchy lately; a man got
flabby riding around in a car all the time when he
wasn't sitting in an office dispensing pills and advice. Fishing was great, when he found the time
for it, but the exercise value was negligible, and
his diet left a great deal to be desired. When you
lived alone, there was no particular incentive to
eat right, even if you were a doctor.

Clare, still looking at him with that new sort of appraisal, said, "I don't have a penny with me, and I imagine the price of thoughts has gone up, like everything else. But even so. . . ."

He found himself stammering again. He said, "I'm sorry." And he wondered, with a flash of wry amusement, what she would say to him if he told her what he actually had been thinking, if he said, "I was wondering how I appear in your eyes, and what you think of me?"

Near-strangers didn't say things like that to each other at cocktail parties; not, at least, without the fortitude provided by a few drinks. Drinks. He discovered his own glass was empty and a quick survey showed him that Clare's was, too.

"Shall we get refills?" he suggested.

She smiled, and he discovered that she had a smile that literally seemed to light her face. She said, "Dr. Casey, you're dodging the issue." She was laughing at him but it was gentle laughter, and for the moment their roles were reversed. For the moment, he felt as if she were the older one, in fact she made him feel like a bungling schoolboy.

They passed Brent Nickerson en route to the bar and he gave Clare a long and appreciative look and said, "Hello, beautiful. Hi, doc."

Greg Banning, talking volubly to a group of people who were all strangers to Casey, smiled his attractively crooked smile and waved affably at both of them.

Tony Mayo and Florence Page had joined a group at the far end of the lawn, and Casey recognized two of the people in it; Hank and Jane Bailey, the husband and wife team who published the *Cape Cod Clarion*, Devon's weekly newspaper.

Barton Smith said, "What'll it be, Mrs. Evans? Doc?"

Clare asked for gin and bitter lemon and Casey requested a Jack Daniels.

"Quite a party," Smith said.

"How many, do you think?" Clare asked.

"Hard to tell," Smith admitted. "Folks leave their glasses around and come back and start from scratch. But I'd guess somewhere between eighty and a hundred."

They moved away and Casey said, "I'm not trying to pry, but if your brother-in-law is as broke as you seem to think he is, this party's going to take quite a toll, isn't it?"

"Yes, if he ever pays Olson's for the liquor and Smith for the catering," Clare acknowledged. "Or maybe Smith orders the liquor from Olson and pays for it himself and then sends Greg the total tab. I don't know which way it goes. If it's the latter, I feel rather sorry for Smith."

"Won't Banning pay him sooner or later?"

"I suppose he'll have to, since he's planning to be a year-round resident," Clare admitted. "But for that, I'd say Smith has got himself a tax loss! Greg doesn't care about things like bills; he seems to think it goes with the so-called artistic temperament to be casual about money matters.

and Carla just goes on spending money whether it's there or not. But God help the establishment that tells her the Banning credit is no longer good. They go directly on the black list, and Carla's great at ruining reputations.''

Clare looked up at him, that appraising look in her eyes again. She said, ''You must think I'm terrible, going on like this about Greg and Carla when I've been living under their roof for three months.''

He said, involuntarily, ''It's been that long?'' and thought, a bit sickeningly, all that time wasted!

''Yes,'' she said. ''I came the Memorial Day weekend. I had no intention of staying on but Carla really seems to need me. Also, although Greg may be a louse as a person and as a husband, he *is* quite an artist. He offered me the chance to paint with him, and he doesn't usually let anyone into his inner circle. Master-student, yes, but this has been pretty much artist-artist, except that I *have* learned. You couldn't have a brush in your hand around Greg and not learn, I'll say that much for him.''

''So, you've been doing quite a bit of painting?''

''Almost every day, except when he's been too hung over. Despite the quantities he consumes of that weird mixture he drinks he seldom does get to the point where he's hung over, though, believe it or not. He says it's his Scandinavian constitution. He's part Norwegian.''

''What *does* he drink?''

"Gin and *cassis*," said Clare. He raised his eyebrows in silent question and she added, "*Cassis* is made from black currants. Personally I find it rather odd tasting. It's popular in France, but mostly as an aperitif mixed with vermouth. Greg's the only person I've ever known who drinks it with gin. He brews it up and stores it in that odd old bottle of his. I think they call it a Poland Springs bottle—it's supposed to be a figure of Moses. Greg says he likes the *cassis* and the gin to age together and then he drinks it on the rocks. It's all a pose, I'm sure. Greg *does* have to be different."

She really doesn't like him, Casey thought, and found the thought strangely comforting. He said, "You're quite knowledgeable about aperitifs and such. Did you study art in France?"

"No," she said. "My husband was very much up on that sort of thing. He was in public relations, and he had a liquor importer among his clients."

She spoke casually enough. Nothing to read, one way or another, in her mention of her husband.

At their elbows, Brent Nickerson said, "Doc, you can't keep her all to yourself." He was almost *too* handsome, dressed in a white jacket with navy slacks and a bright blue shirt, white tie, polished teeth and a smile that he switched on and off like a many-candled chandelier.

"Clare," he said, and turned on a dazzling number of watts, "Carla's just told me that she and Greg actually are going to live here year-round. That means you, too, doesn't it?''

She shook her head. ''No. I'm planning to go back to New York in another week or so.'' She smiled. ''I'm going to have to forgo this life of luxury and find myself a job.''

He frowned in exaggerated dismay. He said, ''New York, necessarily? Boston would be closer.''

''I don't know a soul in Boston.''

''Well, *that* could be remedied easily enough,'' Brent told her with a confidence that Casey was not at all sure was justified. But then, he reasoned, Brent probably needed to build up his ego more than most people, despite his good looks. It was just about a year since his wife had celebrated Labor Day by leaving both Cape Cod and him, driving off with an officer of the same bank Brent worked for. It had been Devon's major scandal of the year.

Clare said lightly, ''I also don't know Boston at all, and I *have* had a couple of offers in New York. I know a lot of people seem to think it's a jungle these days, but I'm comfortable living there.''

She looked out across the lawn and beyond the dunes to the ocean. Casey, following her eyes, saw the straw-gold beach grass swaying gently in the breeze, and watched a gull swoop down to the shallow water, probably to capture a whelk or a moon snail.

Clare said with a certain wistfulness, ''If I had

enough money of my own, and a place of my own, I think I could stay on the Cape forever, but as it is. .." She shrugged, then said, "Maybe someday."

Brent swallowed hard, looking to Casey as if he might be on the verge of a proposal. Or a proposition? Whichever, it was none of his business, Casey told himself sternly and said, "Excuse me," then moved away as if he had suddenly seen someone across the lawn he wanted to talk to.

His path led him to Hank and Jane Bailey, and they spoke for the next few minutes about nothing in particular, in the way of people at cocktail parties who tend to tilt at verbal windmills in the effort of searching for points to make.

Hank Bailey was a dour, dumpy little man, with a habit of rubbing his eyes, as if in a perpetual effort to wake up. He had started the *Cape Cod Clarion* the better part of twenty years ago and he had done a good job with it, but strangely, success seemed to have made him bitter.

Hank had a tart tongue and he was a poor person to get into a discussion with when he'd had a few drinks, as he had now. Casey suspected that much of his trouble came from the fact that he was a frustrated artist.

Occasionally, he still did illustrations for features in his paper, particularly if these dealt with "Olde Cape Cod." But Greg Banning had touched on truth, painful as it might be, when at a dinner party one night he had branded Hank a fifth-rate cartoonist. In view of Hank's violent reaction at the time it seemed odd that the Baileys would have even considered coming to this party, yet that seemed to be the way of Devon, or perhaps, Casey conceded, it was the way of most small communities. In any event, he had long since discovered that it was more usual than unusual for bitter enemies to meet over their martinis, smiling and speaking pleasantries with forked tongues.

There was talk, for example, that Hank at one time had had an affair with Florence Page, this to the point where the Baileys' best friends were taking bets on the chances of a divorce. But the breach had been mended, although there was no way at all of telling how strong the cement was.

There had been talk, too, that Jane had played a summer role in Greg Banning's life one year, and whether this was truth or fiction was a matter of conjecture, but Casey suspected that it might very well be true. Jane was a handsome woman, with strong, aquiline features and dark hair that was swept back from her high, pale forehead and twisted in an ornate French knot. But, like Hank, she was bitter, sour. You could see it in her eyes.

Like Hank, Jane was inclined to drink too much. But again, Casey had to admit, this was par for the course. Alcoholism and infidelity and resulting divorce; these were chronic Cape Cod problems that, according to professional surveys, occurred with at least twice the frequency here than they did on that "mainland" that stretched beyond the two bridges crossing the Cape Cod Canal.

The party progressed and Casey moved from one group to another. Once Carla nearly cornered him, but her attempt was interrupted by a stranger whom she introduced as Robert Fawcett, a tall, prematurely gray-haired man who, she said, was Greg's attorney from New York, come up over Labor Day on a combined business-pleasure weekend.

Banning himself didn't seem to have been upset by the early departure of the Van Houdens. His drinks, though, did seem to be affecting him more obviously then they usually did. He was exuberant, hearty, his deep laugh rang out again and again.

The party reached a saturation point and although the late summer sun was still a way from touching the waters of Cape Cod Bay to the west, people began to leave.

Nature called, and Casey sought out the first floor powder room and, emerging, found Mary Blodgett replenishing the trays of sliced ham, buttered biscuits, and other foods spread out on the damask-covered table in the dining room.

Mary was a gnome of a woman, not nearly as old as she looked, Casey suspected, but gnarled and bent beyond her years from plain hard work. You were apt to run into her anywhere; pinch hitting on the sales force at Fulcher's Bakery or Olson's liquor store or working as a volunteer for the Heart Fund or the Red Cross.

He said, "What now, Mary?"

She grinned. "Going to put out this stuff and leave," she said. "I got to go get Percy's supper."

Dinner to Mary was old Cape Cod style—something you ate at noon, even if that "something" was no more than a tunafish sandwich.

Normally Casey knew, Percy Blodgett would be expecting his supper at approximately five o'clock, so Mary was already on the late side.

She seemed to read his mind. She said, "I got a scalloped clam casserole set to pop in the oven."

"Lucky Percy," said Casey. But Percy, he knew, was not lucky at all.

A few years back, before he, himself, came to Devon, Percy had suffered a severe stroke not long after the Blodgett's only daughter was killed in an automobile accident. For years prior to that Percy had worked in a local hardware store; evidently he still received a small pension. But Mary was the principal breadwinner in the family, keeping things together by spreading herself out in a dozen different directions. In Casey's book, Mary was what one would call a real Cape Codder: tough, resilient, impossible to keep down.

She said, "You ought to try the ham. It ain't half bad."

But Pris Standish, his part-time housekeeper, had cooked a ham for him on Friday, designed to give him "something to have" through the weekend. Since he had gone out to dinner both Friday and Saturday nights he had eaten it for both breakfast and lunch each day.

He suppressed a grimace and said, "Maybe later."

French windows led from the dining room to a side terrace from which a path branched back that led to the front lawn. As he stepped onto the terrace, Casey was facing directly toward Greg Banning's studio just as Carla staggered out of the studio door.

She saw him and came stumbling toward him, pressing her hand over her mouth as she retched, her eyes wide with horror.

5

CASEY'S REACTION WAS AUTOMATIC, instinctive. He covered the distance between them with long strides that could be extremely effective in emergencies. Carla virtually flew at him, and his arms went out to enfold her. She sobbed, "Lon, oh, my God, Lon!"

She was shaking, her teeth were chattering. He said sharply, "Take a long breath. A *long* one! Okay, now, what is it?"

"Greg," she said. She gestured back to the studio. She said, "He's in there." Her face contorted. She said, "I'm going to be sick," and plunged toward the house.

She had left the studio door open, and now Casey's long strides took him through it, and on into the big room with its slanting, skylighted roof. Late shadows were invading, so that despite the expanse of glass the light was dim. It took a moment to adjust his eyes, to see the figure sprawling on the floor next to the oversized studio couch.

Casey crossed to Gregory Banning and knelt by his side, instinctively feeling for a pulse. There still was one, though it was irregular. Banning was breathing heavily; he tossed as if in the grip of a nightmare, mumbling incoherently, clearly delirious. His eyes were open, yet unseeing, the pupils dilated. His face was deeply flushed.

Casey cursed the fact that he had not brought his medical bag with him this afternoon. He almost always put the bag in his car, locking it up because of the drug supply he carried with him that, though modest enough, still could prove quite an incentive to some people.

Today, unfortunately, he had left the bag in his office so, for the moment, there was no accurate way of checking Greg Banning's vital signs. He could only make an educated guess.

Now his long strides took him to the pale blue telephone in the córner. He dialed the emergency police number and told the dispatcher to send out the rescue squad.

A shadow fell across the floor and he looked up. Ironically, it was Tony Mayo. Mayo saw Banning and said, "Christ!" And then, more levelly, "What happened?"

"I'm not sure," Casey said. "It could be a coronary, it could be a stroke, but somehow I don't think it's either. Rescue's on the way. Steer them in here, will you?"

"Right," Tony said, and looking very grim about it, went back out into the day's final, golden sunlight.

Casey returned to Gregory Banning, frustrated because for the moment there was nothing he could do but stare at him.

Why had he come in here, he wondered, and

with whom? A woman? It would be like Banning to have taken a woman to his studio while the party swirled outside.

Casey sniffed. There was no trace of perfume, but then the studio windows were open, the sea breeze had been sweeping through here all afternoon.

On an impulse, he knelt beside Banning and sniffed his breath. He smelled a rather heavy odor of alcohol, but nothing else. This raised another question. Where was the gin mixture that Banning had been drinking? Had he come into the studio without a glass in his hand? This seemed out of character, especially in the midst of a cocktail party.

Casey's eyes roved the floor for a glimpse of a glass, then he lifted the edge of the studio couch cover and was rewarded. Banning obviously had been holding the glass when he fell, and it had rolled just under the edge of the couch where it lay, glinting dully.

Casey carefully picked it up by the edges and sniffed. Again he smelled alcohol. Alcohol and something else he couldn't identify, which was probably the black-currant liqueur that Clare had mentioned.

He got to his feet again just as Bert Higgins, Devon's Chief of Police, walked into the room. Bert was almost as tall as Gregory Banning and lean to the point of gauntness, yet he still gave an impression of hidden strength, which, as it happened, was accurate.

His rugged, homely face showed mingled concern and distaste, which was fairly standard for the chief at moments like this. Surprise surfaced briefly when he saw Casey. He asked, nodding toward Gregory Banning, "He's dead, then?"

"No," said Casey. "At least not yet."

"Then why are you here?"

For the past three years Casey had served as a county medical examiner and he knew that it was this the chief of police was thinking about. He said, "I'm a guest."

Bert nodded. "Rescue's right behind me," he said, and this literally was so. Men came in, and Casey gratefully accepted a bag that contained a stethoscope, among other things, and went to work. Electric lights were turned on; the studio blazed. The chief of police, watching Casey, asked, "Ambulance?" and Casey shook his head.

"They can transport him direct in the rescue truck," he said. "I don't want to wait. Call ahead to the hospital. I'll follow in my own car."

The rescue team worked with steady precision, and Banning already was being hoisted to a stretcher that was almost too short for him.

Bert Higgins said, "Was Tony Mayo a guest here, too?"

Casey nodded, and the chief of police said, "Convenient."

"Don't be such a pessimist."

"Aren't you?"

It was impossible to fool Bert Higgins. Close to impossible, anyway. Casey said, resignedly, "Yes. But we'll see...."

The chief grinned, a twisted grin. "I suppose

there is always hope," he observed, the words touched with cynicism.

"Yes, there is, damn it!"

"Okay, Pete."

Bert Higgins had nicknamed him Pete because his middle name was Pierre, in memory of a French grandfather. His entire name, for that matter, intrigued the chief, who bore the name of an old Cape family himself and marveled that Casey had not somehow also been named Franklin in honor of his mother's side of the family.

As it was, the Casey was self explanatory. It was his first name, Alonzo, that provided the odd note, but he felt it had a Portuguese flavor, which was suitable on Cape Cod where there was a large year-round Portuguese population.

Once Dr. Casey had searched out its meaning, and had retreated in mild confusion. Alonzo, it seemed, was the same as Alphonso, which was in turn the same as Alfonso. Yet Alphonso was listed as Teutonic in origin (where it meant "ready or eager for battle") while Alfonso was listed as of Italian or Spanish derivation (and had been the name of no less than six Portuguese kings!).

Whatever, he was Pete to Chief Bert Higgins.

Higgins asked now, "Any idea how many people were here?"

Casey shook his head. "Quite a few left before this happened," he said, "though I talked to Barton Smith at one point, and he said he thought there had been a total of eighty to a hundred guests."

"Anyone in here with Banning—except you, that is?"

"I wasn't in here with him," Casey said. "I was coming out of the side entrance off the dining room just as Carla ran out of here looking as if the devil was on her heels. She told me he was in here."

"How did she say it, do you remember?"

"Just 'Greg—he's in there,' I think. Then she said she was going to be sick and she bolted into the house. From her color at the moment I'd say she very probably *was* sick."

"So she didn't come out and say Banning was dead?"

"No."

Bert Higgins nodded heavily. A siren sounded. The rescue squad was starting out for the Cape Cod Hospital in Hyannis.

Dr. Casey said, "I've got to get going."

Bert Higgins nodded. He said, "I'll be in touch later." His homely face was etched with gloom. "Let's hope he lives."

6

GREGORY BANNING DID NOT LIVE. Shortly after 2:00 A.M. Dr. Casey took the elevator down to the hospital waiting area, where Carla huddled with her sister, and led the two women into the small meditation room that had been set aside for friends and relatives of patients.

Fortunately it was empty. He closed the door behind them and said slowly, "Carla, I'm sorry. It's all over."

She looked at him dully. Although she seemed totally sober, now, he had the feeling that she hadn't understood him and he was about to repeat himself when she said, "I know, Lon. I know."

Clare's lovely face was wooden. This is hitting home to her, Casey thought. It isn't that long since she lost her own husband.

He said gently, "Carla, Tony Mayo's here. He'll take care of everything. You can talk to him later."

She nodded like an obedient child.

"I'm going to drive you both home," he said.

Clare spoke. "I'll drive her," she said. "We came over in my car."

"Tony can take your car back to Devon," said Casey. "Give me the keys, and I'll get them to him. Just now, I think you'd better leave the driving to me."

Clare shrugged, her indifference making him feel foolish. Doubtless, he was underestimating her. Doubtless, she was made of far sterner stuff than he assumed, and was more than capable of taking her sister back to the house on The Heights. But in any event . . . .

He found Tony Mayo and gave him Clare's car keys, then shepherded the two women out to his own car, which he had pulled up just beyond the front entrance. Carla and Clare were silent, taut. On the way back to Devon, the three of them said very little to each other.

He stopped briefly at his office to pick up his medical bag, then drove on to The Heights. It was still dark, but there was a morning touch to the breeze that stung their cheeks as they walked from the car into the house; a freshness.

There were lights on in the dining room and in the kitchen beyond, but the rest of the place was in darkness. Clare took the initiative now. She went ahead into the living room and switched on lamps, while Carla slumped down on a sofa.

Looking around the room, Casey noted that someone had cleaned it up. Ashtrays had been emptied, pillows plumped back into place. He wondered if the lawn outside and Barton Smith's bar had already been tidied, too.

For that matter, he wondered who was out in the kitchen right now, for he had heard sounds as they walked in. Someone, he thought, was washing dishes.

Clare said, "Would you like a drink, doctor?"

"Yes," he said. "Carla, some brandy, perhaps?"

She raised lackluster eyes. "Anything," she said.

"I'll get it," he said to Clare. "What about you, gin and bitter lemon?"

She smiled faintly. "No, thanks. Brandy, too, I think. And I imagine it's Barton Smith out in the kitchen."

Their eyes met. You are sharp, lady, he thought. Are you, perhaps, even a mind reader? But he said only, "Well, he can do the bartending, then."

Barton Smith *was* in the kitchen, but he was not alone. Mary Blodgett was with him, washing glasses while Barton dried them and stashed them away in the cartons he had brought with him, this a part of his catering service.

They looked up as Dr. Casey came in and simultaneously formed the same question.

"How's Mr. Banning?"

"He didn't make it," Casey said briefly.

Mary gasped, and Barton Smith whistled softly.

Mary said, "Poor Mrs. Banning! Where is she?"

"In the living room with her sister. Barton, can you rustle up three king-sized brandies?"

"Sure."

"The brandy glasses are in that glass cabinet in the dining room," Mary told him.

"That's okay. I got some of my own," Barton replied.

He set out the glasses, found a bottle, poured. He said, "What was it? Heart?"

"We don't know yet," Casey evaded.

Mary was shaking her head. "Here one minute, gone the next," she said.

Barton Smith nodded solemnly. "Never saw him look better," he avowed. "He was in top shape all evening. *Enjoying* himself, a little high, maybe, but Jesus. . . ."

"Had he been drinking more than usual?" Casey asked.

Barton Smith thought this over. He came to a conclusion. "I wouldn't say so," he decided. "He could pack it away, but then he was a big guy. Not that *that* always proves anything. I've seen little guys who could drink big guys under the table. But Banning, well, at least from what I've seen of him, he was kind of a *consistent* drinker, if you follow me."

"Did it usually hit him quite the way it did tonight?" Casey asked. "I mean, I noticed myself that he was riding high."

Barton Smith thought this over, too. "I couldn't say," he finally admitted. "I was pouring out the drinks as fast as I could handle them, doc. Hundreds of them during the course of the party. Mr. Banning kept coming back for a slug out of that fancy bottle of his every now and then. After a while he wasn't feeling any pain, I can tell you that, and everything anybody said seemed to strike him funny. . . ."

He paused, and Casey said, "Yes?"

"Well, come to think of it, I'd never seen him

quite like *that* before. He wasn't any jokester, usually. You know what I mean? I'd say he was the type to get a little on the ugly side after a few drinks. But not tonight.''

''Bart,'' Mary Blodgett began reproachfully, ''you shouldn't talk like that. He's dead.''

''He's only answering what I asked him, Mary,'' Dr. Casey told her. ''What about Banning's bottle, by the way?''

''I put it back in the cabinet in the dining room,'' said Mary Blodgett. ''That's where he usually kept it.''

''You've worked here before, Mary?''

She nodded. ''Once in a while, when Mrs. Banning has a dinner party or something. Bart caters, usually, and he calls me in to help serve table. Mrs. Banning's no cook, I guess.''

Bart Smith laughed. ''You can say that again! She told me once that she just barely managed to learn how to open a can.''

''Bertha Murphy comes in to do the cleaning and the washing and ironing,'' Mary volunteered, ''but Bertha ain't much of a cook, either. Matter of fact, I don't see how she does much of anything. She's got so fat she starts wheezing if she walks up a flight of stairs.''

Casey laughed. ''People don't often come as streamlined as you are, Mary,'' he teased her.

Clare, in the doorway, said, ''Could I help with those brandies?''

Casey felt as if he'd suddenly run a temperature, and he wondered if his face was visibly red.

He said, ''I'm sorry.''

"Quite all right," said Clare, and accepted the glass of brandy he handed her.

He carried the other two, following her back into the living room, and she said softly, "I don't know whether Carla's going to fall asleep or suddenly go into hysterics."

Carla was precisely where he had left her, still slumped in the corner of a long couch, staring vacantly at the blue and green pattern of the wall-to-wall carpeting.

He gave her the brandy and said, "Come on, Carla, sip some of this." She obeyed, looking across at him over the rim of the glass and suddenly her eyes filled with tears. She stood, setting the glass aside, and stumbled toward him, and he obligingly set his own glass aside and put his arms around her. "It's all right," he murmured. "Go ahead and cry. Cry all you want."

He glanced across at Clare and surprised a peculiar expression on her face; disbelief, that was the only thing he could think to call it, which seemed odd under the circumstances. Carla sobbed, "Lon, how can I go on living? It was my fault, I *drove* him to it!"

He frowned. "To what, Carla?"

"To killing himself," she wailed.

He stepped back, staring down at her. The thought of Gregory Banning having committed suicide had not entered his mind. Certainly the Banning he had seen tonight had not been suicidal—he would stake his professional reputation on that.

He said, "Carla. . .I doubt Greg killed himself."

He took a folded handkerchief out of his pocket and handed it to her, and she daubed furiously at her eyes.

"Then what happened?" she asked him.

"I don't know yet," he said slowly. "We shall have to have an autopsy."

The wide gray eyes were shocked and the shock was honest; this, certainly, she was not feigning. She moaned, "Oh, no!"

And Clare said sharply, "Isn't that up to Carla, Dr. Casey?"

He shook his head reluctantly. "I'm afraid not. I'm afraid in this particular case it is up to me. I'm a county medical examiner."

Again, he could think of only a single word to describe her expression; this time it was distaste. He said, steeling himself, "I can't possibly issue a death certificate until I am satisfied as to the precise cause of death."

"And you're not?" Clare asked him.

"I'm not," he said.

Their eyes locked. War, he thought, and wondered why.

He took a healthy swig of his brandy, then said, "Carla, my bag's out in my car. I'm going to get it, and in the meantime I want Clare to take you up to your room and get you ready for bed."

"I can't possibly go to bed, Lon," she protested.

"Yes, you can," he told her. "I'm going to give you a shot so you'll sleep for a few hours. That's what you need more than anything else right now."

She did not dispute this, and Clare said, "Come on, Carla."

They were starting up the stairs as he went out to his car. He unlocked the back, took out his black bag and made his way back to the house through a starless night.

Clare had turned on a single bed-table lamp in Carla's room, which was in every sense a boudoir, Casey thought, looking at the frilly curtains, pillows, and Carla herself, seductive in a lilac nightgown despite her sorrow.

He gave her the shot, promised he'd stop by in the morning, then went back downstairs. A moment later Clare followed.

She seemed pale, intensely preoccupied, but still she said, politely, "You haven't finished your brandy, doctor."

"Nor have you," he reminded her.

They sat in low armchairs across from each other, and Clare said, "This autopsy. When will it take place?"

"Sometime this morning, I hope," he said. "Chief Higgins has put in a call for a state pathologist to come down."

"Then you don't do it yourself?"

He looked at her levelly. "I could. But no, I usually don't. It's preferable, at least in my opinion—and I think most of the medical examiners agree with me—to have a state pathologist on hand."

"When this has been done will you know immediately what caused Greg's death?"

"That's impossible to say," Casey evaded. "It depends on so many things."

Clare nodded stiffly, "I suppose so," she conceded.

She walked to the door with him. Her head came just above his shoulder, and he found himself wishing that he had met her at another time, in other circumstances, in a completely different place.

He said, "This may upset your own plans. Going back to New York, I mean. Carla will probably want you to stay here with her for a time."

"I don't know," she said. "She may want to close this place and come back to the city with me. But that remains to be seen."

He hesitated. "Clare," he said then, "I'm sorry."

She looked up at him, surprised. "About what?" she asked him.

"The need for an autopsy, among other things. I noticed your reaction, I can understand it, but there are those things that I'm forced to do. Can you understand *that*?"

"Yes," she said slowly. "Yes, I can." And she added, "I wouldn't want to be in your position."

7

ONCE IN HIS YELLOW STATION WAGON, Casey found himself brooding about his own role in the previous night's events, first as a party-goer, then as a doctor, finally as a medical examiner. He thought of Clare Evans's reaction to this latter capacity and winced a little, and then for a time he thought about Clare. Finally he stopped thinking entirely and drove across town to Jessie's Kitchen, and this morning the warmth and friendliness of the small, pine-panelled restaurant seemed more important than ever.

BERT HIGGINS WAS SITTING at a table in the corner, and the doctor joined him. Jessie left the counter where she usually presided and came across to serve him personally, and when he had given his order Bert Higgins said, "She doesn't do that for me."

"Charm," Casey said succinctly. He started to reach into his coat pocket for his pipe and then remembered that he was still wearing the jacket he had worn to the party, and so didn't have it.

Bert said, "Looking for that smelly old briar again?"

Casey nodded, and the police chief said, scowling, "It'll harm you!"

"A pipe's the least harmful. . . ." Casey began. Then he grinned, despite himself. "Okay," he admitted. "I should know better."

Bert Higgins smiled, satisfied. Then, sobering, he said, "What do we have here?"

They had worked together before. Dr. Casey knew precisely what he meant. He said, "I don't know."

"I know *you*," said the police chief. "You've got ideas."

"Only ideas. . . so far."

Joanie, the waitress, said at his elbow, "More coffee, Chief?" and Bert Higgins nodded. She filled his cup, and said, "Coffee for you, Dr. Casey?"

He said, "Yes, please." As he stirred a scant teaspoonful of sugar into his coffee, he said, "Hindsight's always great, of course. It was by pure accident, really, that I was there at all. How I wish I had paid more attention to Banning! I didn't see that much of him. When I got there, he was in his studio with some wealthy, would-be patrons. Later, I spotted him from time to time, you could hardly help it. He was loud; he laughed a lot."

"Didn't he ordinarily?"

"Not in the same way." Casey frowned. "You'll be talking to the various guests, I suppose?"

"I guess so."

"Well, try to get their impressions of Banning.

Try to find out who saw him last, and if he was alone when he went back into his studio."

"Would you like to take over the investigation for me?" Higgins asked with deceptive politeness.

"Hell, no," said Casey. "I've got enough to do without playing policeman."

Higgins said, "It's Labor Day. It's supposed to be a holiday."

Casey smiled wryly. "Not for such as you and I. I still have house calls to make, and the office after that."

Jessie brought French toast and crisp bacon and put it down before him. She said, "If you want anything else, just call."

Bert Higgins said, "I think she went out in the kitchen and cooked that herself!" Then, seriously, "What about Mrs. Banning and her sister?"

"What about them?"

"Are you planning to see them later?"

"Yes, as a matter of fact. I have a patient out on The Heights—old Tim Fotherington, his heart's been kicking up lately. I thought I'd stop at the Bannings after I see him. Why?"

"Just thought maybe you could pass along any information you could get from them," said Bert Higgins. "You know, this is kind of awkward. It's a police matter, and yet isn't. Sudden death, yes. But it could, maybe, have been a coronary or a cerebral hemorrhage or something like that, even if you don't seem to think so."

"I suppose it *could* have been," Casey admitted.

"Yeah," said Higgins. "You *suppose*. Could have been suicide, too, couldn't it?"

"That I doubt."

"Why?"

"In my opinion, Banning wasn't the suicidal type."

"Then what you're telling me," said the chief, "is that the chances are this is murder, right?"

"Yes."

"Since he wasn't shot, wasn't stabbed, wasn't strangled, wasn't hit over the head, that leaves poison, right?"

"Possibly."

"What kind of poison?"

Dr. Casey smiled. "I'm not a walking toxicologist," he admitted mildly.

"Maybe you're not, but you know a hell of a lot more about stuff like that than I do," Higgins said, "and even I can eliminate some of them. It wasn't cyanide or strychnine or barbiturates or lye, or anything like that."

"No."

"So what could it have been?"

Casey shrugged. "Bert," he said, "you know as well as I do that there are all kinds of poisons. I couldn't even begin to give you an accurate count. Also, it's been a long time since I've hit the textbooks. You can't remember them all. But what sticks in my mind is the smell of alcohol."

"Are you saying maybe he drank himself to death?"

"No. Drinking oneself to death doesn't work out that way, as you also damn well know. No,

I'm saying, and this is strictly off the record, that I'd be inclined to suspect alcohol poisoning. Remember prohibition?''

"I'm getting older," Higgins conceded, "but I'm not *that* old.''

"Neither am I. But we've both read books and seen movies. The gangster days, flappers, bootleg gin—sometimes methyl alcohol by mistake, and people would die or go blind.''

"You think—methyl alcohol?''

"I don't think *anything*," Casey said firmly. "I'm just guessing out loud. When I get back to the office I'm going to do a little research with my *Materia Medica*. But even if it bears me out, there's no way we can be sure till we get some lab results.''

"That," said Higgins gloomily, "could take forever.''

"Patience, Bertram," said Casey, and grinned as the chief silently mouthed a four-letter word at him.

THE DRIVEWAY THAT LED to Dr. Casey's house and his adjacent office was so constructed that by driving around to the back of the house one could park out of sight of Fuller Road. Casey had learned to employ this bit of subterfuge on occasion, and he did so now. Leaving the car in the front driveway was tantamount to putting up a billboard stating, The Doctor Is at Home.

He went first to his office, paused briefly to pick up his *Materia Medica*, and then took it into the house with him, heading directly for the kitchen where he filled the coffeepot and plugged it in.

While the coffee was perking, he turned to the section on "Brain and Spinal Cord Depressants."

There it was—methyl alcohol. Chemical formula CH_3OH.

Until the late 1920s, when a new method had been invented, methyl alcohol, more commonly known as wood alcohol, had been manufactured by the destructive distillation of wood. Very possibly, Casey thought, it still might be, in some areas. But principally it was produced now from natural gas or coal. With either procedure, a colorless liquid was obtained that tasted like drinking alcohol. Thus it was that during the prohibition years in the United States unscrupulous individuals had not hesitated to sell wood alcohol as the real thing, with the result of either blindness or death for the individual who drank it.

The shelf life was indefinite; if anything, the older the methyl alcohol, the stronger it became.

And, yes, it was a violent poison, no doubt about that. Death could be caused by even prolonged inhalation of the stuff. Or, the imbibing of as little as a few ounces.

And the symptoms. Absently, Dr. Casey poured a cup of coffee and stirred sugar into it as he read, "The symptoms begin like an ordinary alcoholic intoxication with excitement and exhilaration. This is followed by nausea, vomiting, dizziness, headache, dilated pupils and delirium. Persistent coma and death may follow within a few hours or a few days."

So. Gregory Banning had been excited, exhilarated, louder than usual. Had he begun to feel nauseated, dizzy? Was that why he had gone back into his studio?

Dr. Casey closed the book, drank his coffee, and started to think about the party and the people and Greg Banning. But not for long. The phone began to ring. He frowned and answered it, and it was a patient.

No. Labor Day was not, necessarily, a holiday.

8

DR. GEORGE WILLIAMS, a state pathologist with whom Dr. Casey had worked on prior occasions, was spending the Labor Day weekend with friends in Chatham. He agreed to perform the autopsy on Gregory Banning, and this, in a sense, was a bonanza. Definitely, it meant saved time.

The autopsy was scheduled for 10:00 A.M. at the Parkington Funeral Home. Dr. Williams did his usual thorough job and said the usual things once it was over, which principally added up to the fact that everything would be sent to Boston for analysis.

Casey nodded agreement, but nevertheless posed a question.

"Poison?" he asked.

"Off the record, I'd say so."

"Methyl alcohol, perhaps?"

Dr. Williams pursed his lips. "Perhaps."

Bert Higgins, a captive spectator, groaned. "You guys don't believe in talking too much, do you?" he observed caustically.

"We can't *say*, Chief," Dr. Williams pointed out.

"Shit," said Higgins, "you could give an educated guess."

"I think we both just did," Casey said. And Dr. Williams nodded.

"The body can be released," Casey added. "No point holding things up. We have everything we need."

"I hope so," Bert Higgins said doubtfully.

Dr. Williams, washing his hands, then wiping them on a towel, said, "If you get anything else don't call me, okay?"

"Right." Casey laughed.

Dr. Williams left them, and Casey waited for Bert Higgins, who paused to consult briefly with Tony Mayo. The two men walked together to the police cruiser parked at the curb.

"Have you been back to see Carla Banning and her sister?" Higgins asked.

Casey shook his head. "I had patients for more than an hour. Then I closed shop and came here. I *should* go back to the office for a while before I do anything else."

Higgins said, "Something kooky happened."

He was frowning, and Casey knew from prior experience that whatever had happened had made the chief unhappy. He asked the obvious question, and Higgins said, "I've been having one of the cruisers check the Banning place at regular intervals. Just routine. They go along Heights Road about as far as the Culkins place, turn down to where you get that good view of the whole beach, and then head back to town."

"I parked down there myself for a few minutes this morning," Dr. Casey conceded.

"Well, John Sears, he's pretty new on the force, pulled in there around 7:00 A.M. He said he shut off the cruiser motor and just sat for a minute, taking a breather. Couldn't believe the beach was all that empty. Sears said from where he sat he could see that flight of steps that goes down from the Banning house and there wasn't a soul around."

"So?" Casey asked.

"Well, he was about to start the motor up again when he saw someone starting down those steps. He doesn't know the names of any of these people, but from his description there's no doubt it was Clare Evans."

Clare. Casey's heart thudded. He said, trying to be reasonable about this, "I imagine she felt she had to get out of the house, which isn't surprising. Probably wanted to walk the beach for a while. I sedated Carla. She would have been asleep."

"It was more than that," Bert Higgins said reluctantly. "Sears watched her; he thought like you she was probably just going for a walk on the beach. She got to the bottom of the steps and started walking all right, but after a while she turned in toward the dunes, and he couldn't figure out what she was doing. It was like she was burrowing in the sand, he said."

"Burrowing?"

"Yes. Digging in."

"Did he pursue it?" Casey asked evenly.

"Yes. After a while she finished and went on back. Seems he waited awhile, then he went down the Culkins's steps and kept close to the dunes so he couldn't be seen from the Banning place, till he got to the spot where she'd been digging. She'd camouflaged it damned well. Put back twigs and dried up seaweed and all the rest. He said if you hadn't been looking for it you would have gone by a thousand times without noticing anything had been disturbed."

"So," Casey said, "I presume that Sears dug?"

"Yes, and he found a bottle. An odd-looking bottle. Shaped like some kind of an old man with a flowing beard."

The Moses bottle.

A YEAR AND A HALF AGO, Devon's new municipal complex had been opened. The town office building, police headquarters, fire department, and the town library now shared spacious quarters on the corner of Doane Parkway and Bay Street, just a block or so away from Devon's geographical center, this formed by the intersection of Route 6A and Main Street.

Bert Higgins's new office in police headquarters was a study in tones of brown and beige with bright orange accents, and he always seemed uncomfortable in it. In the old days, when police headquarters had been in a crowded little building on Main Street, he had been accustomed to leaning back in his swivel chair and putting his feet up on his old wooden, battle-scarred desk. But not now.

It was Dr. Casey who now sat negligently on the edge of the shining new desk, with Higgins, stiff as a ramrod, seated in the chair behind it. Both of them stared intently at the bottle that stood precisely in the center of the chief's cocoa-colored blotter.

The bottle was, indeed, shaped like an old man. A jade green, it depicted Moses, with a staff and a flowing beard.

"Old, I guess," the chief said morosely.

"Probably," Casey conceded. "I don't know too much about bottles, but Eleanor Chase does. I'll ask her. Matter of fact, I think I have one of these."

"*You?*"

"Aunt Agatha's," Casey said briefly. "She saved everything, collected everything."

He remembered Clare telling him about the bottle yesterday. What had she called it? "That odd, old bottle of Greg's."

A pose, she had said. Greg drinking his gin and *cassis* out of a special old bottle was a pose, because Greg had to be different.

Bert Higgins said, "Ask Eleanor about it, will you?"

"Yes."

"And . . . Pete?"

"Yes?"

"Don't say anything at the Banning house about Sears finding this."

Casey raised his eyebrows. "Do you think you really had to tell me that?"

"No," Bert Higgins said uncomfortably. Then, "Okay, I don't like this one."

Casey did not like this one, either. Why Clare, he asked himself, as he drove from police headquarters out to The Heights. He could not believe that she had poisoned Greg Banning. In fact, he would find it impossible to believe that she could willfully harm anyone; and even as he started to follow this line of reasoning he broke it off abruptly and told himself not to be a damned fool.

So she seemed to him a very lovely person, underneath that sometimes tense exterior; there was a certain quality about her that attracted him, and he wasn't about to deny it. But he also was not, for God's sake, so naive as to believe that this precluded the possibility of her having mixed methyl alcohol with that black currant stuff—*cassis*, that was the name of it—and having poured it into the Moses bottle for Greg's consumption. The mere fact that she had tried to hide the bottle denoted something.

Carla was in the living room, wearing a pale blue caftan that made her seem disarmingly fragile. She was fondling a tall, frosted glass. She said, "Lon, I just mixed myself a gin and tonic. Join me?"

He shook his head, noting that it was barely noon. Not that she didn't have more excuse than usual today. But even so. . . .

He said, forcing a smile, "My sun isn't over the yardarm yet."

Carla made a face at him. Then she said, soberly enough, "Tony Mayo called. He's coming by. Arrangements." She added, with disconcerting directness, "What happened?"

He hedged. He said, "We're still not quite sure. We won't be until certain analyses have been completed, and that takes awhile."

She shivered. "I hate funerals."

"Most of us do," Casey said, then asked, "where's Clare?"

"Upstairs, talking to someone in New York," Carla replied. "It's about that job she's going to take, I think. I told her I don't want to go back to the city with her, I really don't, but she doesn't feel she should leave me here."

"When was she going?"

"Next week. Now I think she's suggesting sometime after the fifteenth."

A thought struck him. "They're working today?"

"Who?" Carla asked.

"Whoever it is that Clare will be working for in New York. This is Labor Day."

"So it is," said Carla. "I don't know. I mean, whether they're working in New York or not. Maybe Clare's calling whoever it is at home." She faced him, "Lon, let's not talk around in circles. What *difference* does it make?"

He saw the look in her eyes and mentally ducked, and decided that she was not behaving at all as one would expect a grieving widow to behave. He had the feeling that it would take a very slight suggestion to get Carla into bed with him; it was that obvious.

He backed away from the thought, there was a pause, and she dropped her eyes, then with a slight shrug, sat down on the couch, contemplated her drink and sampled it.

Casey said, "Might there be some coffee in the kitchen?"

"There might be. Mrs. Murphy's out there. She insisted on coming in when she heard about Greg—Labor Day and all." Carla started to rise. "I'll check."

"No," he said quickly, "I can get it myself," and before she could protest he was out of the room and into the dining room, which was precisely where he wanted to be.

There was a cabinet in the corner, with glass doors, and Mary Blodgett had said that she had put the Moses bottle back in there. Now Casey crossed the room in a circuitous way so that he could stop and peer, and it took only a second to establish a fact.

The Moses bottle was right where it belonged!

Without taking it out of the cabinet it was impossible to see how full it was, but that didn't matter too much just now. What *did* matter was the fact that this clearly established that there were two Moses bottles. And that led to some very interesting possibilities.

Mrs. Murphy had coffee ready, and she filled a large mug for him. He took it back to the living room, and found that Clare had joined her sister. She wore jeans this morning and a pullover white sweater, and she looked like a high-school girl, so young, so vulnerable, that it made him ache.

He thought of the Moses bottle on Bert Higgins's desk, finding this a memory that he did not like to harbor. He forced casualness and said, "Good morning."

Clare was not happy to see him. This message, though unspoken, came across clearly. She said, "Good morning, doctor," and they were both saved from taking it further by the telephone's ringing.

It was on an end table at the far end of the couch, and Clare moved to it before Carla could. Dr. Casey saw her jaw tense as she listened, and when she spoke, it was in monosyllables. "Very well. Of course. I'll tell my sister."

She hung up. Her blue eyes were blazing. She said, "The chief of police, Carla. He says an officer from the County Identification Office is on his way here to go over Greg's studio. He wants to check for fingerprints and such, and there will be one of the local police officers with him. The chief hopes you won't object."

Casey concentrated on his coffee. So, Higgins was wasting no time. But he was taking a low-keyed approach, as he always did when there was a choice.

He could *feel* Clare's blue eyes upon him. She said icily, "Was this your idea, doctor?"

Startled, he replied, honestly enough, "No."

Carla said, "What are you talking about, Clare?" She looked from her sister to Dr. Casey and said, "Must you two always *confront* each other? Isn't everything enough of a mess as it is?"

She stared moodily at her glass, now empty. She said, "Oh, hell!" And then, "What do the police want with fingerprints in Greg's studio?''

Clare, her eyes still on Casey, said, "That's for them to say. Or perhaps Dr. Casey could tell us.''

"He's already said he doesn't know what happened to Greg,'' said Carla, which was not, Casey conceded, strictly accurate. She stood up. "I'm going to get another drink before Tony Mayo gets here,'' she said, and headed for the kitchen.

Clare said bitterly, "She drinks too damned much. I suppose she has an excuse today, if ever. But even so, she drinks too much *all* the time. You're her doctor. Can't you do something about it?''

Casey put down his coffee cup. He said, levelly, "You've got it in for me this morning, haven't you?''

"Am I that transparent?''

He smiled wryly. "You can answer that question yourself,'' he said. "As you can also answer the question about whether or not I've tried to do anything about Carla's drinking. Of course I have. I've warned her of the almost inevitable consequences if she keeps on as she's going, just as any doctor would. But I know, and I'm sure you know, that the only person who can do anything about Carla's drinking is Carla, so let's not pursue that particular course at the moment. More important—I'd like to know just what you're blaming me for.''

"Blaming you?'' She shrugged. She went to the window, stood looking out over the ocean. The garish sky that had dominated the east early that morning had changed to pure gray, darker in the distance. There was a satin touch to the ocean. Bad weather coming, definitely.

Clare said, "I don't know. It's just your *being* here, I suppose."

He winced, just as she swung around to look at him. She said, quickly contrite, "I'm sorry. I didn't mean it the way it must have sounded. What I do mean. . .."

"Yes?"

"Well, it's disconcerting to have someone around who is both official and unofficial. You were a guest at the party, after all. Or so I thought."

"Your sister invited me to the party," he pointed out. "I didn't particularly want to go. I don't like cocktail parties. Not that kind, anyway."

A faint smile touched her lips. She said, "Neither do I."

"I certainly didn't ask for a situation where I'd have to start functioning as a medical examiner, if that's what you mean by official," he persisted. "I wasn't here as a doctor, either, if *that's* what you mean by official. Not yesterday, anyway. This morning, well, I suppose that I am here in a dual capacity. I've been acting as Carla's doctor when she's been on the Cape, yes; that's why I sedated her last night, and why I came back now. To see how she is doing—"

Carla, in the doorway, said, "Are you two still at it?" She came into the room, drink in hand, and resumed her position on the couch. She said,

"The police have arrived, and they're out in Greg's studio."

She looked across at Dr. Casey, "They'd like you to join them, Lon," she said.

9

Dr. Casey walked slowly from the main house across the intervening space to Greg Banning's studio. His summons seemed to have confirmed Clare's thoughts about him, and her attitude puzzled him. When, reluctantly, he had asked to be excused, she had looked at him with something very close to dislike.

Why? He admitted—this ruefully—that there had been nothing in their relationship so far to make him seem particularly attractive to her. In fact, on their previous encounters she had not reacted to him at all. But now, especially since learning that he was a medical examiner, she was wary, at moments even hostile.

Also—he reminded himself and didn't like it— she *had* hidden the Moses bottle.

There was an obvious conclusion.

Clare was running scared.

Barney Parker, the fingerprint expert from the County Identification Office, and John Sears were in the process of going over every inch of Banning's studio, slowly, painfully, missing nothing.

Parker said, "We found a glass in an odd spot.

Top shelf, next to some turpentine and linseed oil.''

"I know," Casey said. "I put it there yesterday after I came in here and found Banning on the floor. It was just under the edge of the studio couch—and yes, I was careful how I handled it.''

Parker said, "Plenty of prints on it. Mostly smudged, though there are a couple that might do for a positive. Probably Banning's.''

Casey said, "There's a bottle in the house, in a cabinet in the dining room. Green. A figure of a bearded man. . . .''

Parker stared at him. "Higgins turned one of those over to us for dusting and analysis of the contents," he said.

"Yes, I know he did. Evidently Banning had two of them, and we know he kept the private brew he drank in at least one of them. It's a mixture of gin and a black currant liqueur called *cassis*. Anyway, you ought to go over the bottle in the dining room, too.''

"Will do," Barney Parker said cheerfully. He glanced around the studio. "Quite a place, this," he observed. "He's got one of those stove-refrigerator-sink combinations back of that bamboo screen over there in the corner, and a well-stocked bar, to say nothing of his king-sized studio couch. You could live in this place," Parker decided.

"I guess Banning did sometimes," Casey said dryly.

There was an intercom in the studio, and now it buzzed. Casey pressed the proper button and

Clare's voice came across, cool and totally impersonal.

"There's a call for Mr. Parker," she said. "The C.I.O. says to tell him there has been an accident on the Mid Cape Highway near the Dennis turnoff, and they would like him there as soon as he has finished here."

"Ask her to tell them I'll be right along," Parker said, and Casey relayed the message.

John Sears said, "Doc, the chief wants me to get a list of the people who were at the party last night."

Dr. Casey considered this. "I suppose Mrs. Banning may have one." He turned to the C.I.O. man. "Need any help here, Parker?"

"No," said Barney Parker. "I don't think there's anything except the glass Banning was drinking out of. I'll finish up and get going."

"Then I'll go back to the house with you, Sears," Casey said, "and we'll see about the list."

CARLA BANNING DID NOT HAVE a guest list. "I just kept calling people," she said vaguely. "Greg called some of the people himself, I suppose you could say the whole thing grew like Topsy. That's the way our parties usually do."

John Sears was swallowing hard, and Casey repressed a smile. Although Carla's pale blue caftan was voluminous it was fashioned of sheer material that draped well, and thus was quite revealing, and Carla, a fresh drink in her hand, had curled up on the couch in a position that was decidedly seductive.

Sears, striving to stick to business, said, "Have you *any* idea how many people you and your husband invited, Mrs. Banning?"

"No," said Carla. "A lot, that's all."

Dr. Casey said, "Maybe we could start with the local people. The Baileys, Brent Nickerson, Tony Mayo—"

"Tony should be here pretty soon," Carla said.

"Yes," said Casey. "Look, Carla, I can remember some of the people who were here but only a fraction of them, but perhaps if we all try we can put a list together. You, Clare, me, Tony when he gets here."

Clare, sitting in a corner chair, said, "I really don't know that many people, doctor. The ones you mentioned, of course, and also the artist— Florence Page, isn't it? Then, there were the people Greg wanted to hire him—the Van Houdens—"

"They weren't guests," Carla interrupted. "They just came. That is, Greg asked them to come at the last minute. Not to the party, to talk business. They were in the studio with him the whole time they were here, and that wasn't very long."

"What about Greg's lawyer?" Casey asked.

"Bob Fawcett. He's still here on the Cape—he called earlier. He was planning to go to Provincetown today and I told him to go ahead. He's coming for a drink later this afternoon, and we can talk then about whatever we have to talk about." Carla devoted attention to her drink, and then she said, "Why don't we start with the hired help? Isn't it always the butler who did it? You're acting, Lon, as if somebody killed Greg, and I think that's being rather ridiculous."

"Possibly it is," Dr. Casey said mildly, and did not look at Clare.

"Well, Mrs. Murphy was here earlier, helping get things ready. Mary Blodgett was around most of the time—she works for Barton Smith on things like that. But Bart Smith was the closest thing to a butler we had. He was the bartender." Carla giggled. "Why don't you talk to him?"

Dr. Casey, a sudden note of steel in his voice, said, "What about you, Carla?"

She straightened and looked at him, her gray eyes wide. "Just what do you mean by that?"

"You, aside from myself, were the last person to be with Greg in the studio. How did you happen to go in there?"

Carla sniffed. She said, "Florence Page told me he was sick."

"When?"

"Oh, God, Lon, I don't keep a mental stopwatch going," Carla said impatiently. "I wasn't in the studio very long, though. When I went in he was lying on the floor and twitching, and he looked *terrible*. His eyes were wide open and he was staring right at me, but I had the feeling he didn't see me. Just looking at him made me feel like I was going to be sick, and so I rushed out and ran into you."

"Exactly what did Florence Page say to you?"

"About Greg? Well, I was talking to some people, some of Greg's artist friends from New York who planned to drive back last night. They were looking for Greg, they wanted to say good-bye to him, but they didn't see him around so they came over to say goodbye to me. Just then Florence came up and told me she had to speak to me, she looked so white and funny that I excused myself and we walked away from the others. Florence said she'd just left Greg in the studio and she thought he was very sick." Carla's eyes narrowed. "I wonder why she didn't go right for you," she told Dr. Casey.

"I was in the house," Casey said. "Maybe she did look around for me."

"Well, what was she doing out in the studio with Greg in the first place? Or need I ask?"

Clare said shortly, "Carla, don't conjecture."

It was almost a command, and three pairs of eyes swung toward her. She said, facing all of them, "Guessing doesn't do any good. It would be better to simply ask Florence, and I'm sure Officer Sears, here, will do exactly that—as, no doubt, will Dr. Casey."

I am definitely not her favorite person, Casey thought grimly. But there was a new edge to the thought.

Clare, it was true, had seemed somewhat remote ever since they had met, and he had supposed that this was because she was still grieving over her husband's death. But was she really?

There had been what old-fashioned folks would call a decent interval, more than enough

time for Clare to finish her weeping and dry her
tears, so possibly it was not the late Mr. Evans
who caused her preoccupation but, rather, Greg
Banning.

Perhaps Clare had fallen in love with Banning a
long time ago, as a young art student. Perhaps
this summer had rekindled a romance that, as
such romances sometimes do, had culminated in
hate.

Again he could pinpoint her evident dislike
toward him almost to the moment when she had
found out that he was a county medical examiner. Did this symbolize a police alliance in her
mind, and even if it did, why had it turned her so
decidedly against him?

What did she have to hide?

This question inevitably brought back the
memory of the Moses bottle she had hidden. Why
had she hidden it? He wished he could ask her,
and knew he couldn't for this was Bert Higgins's
territory, not his. Lieutenant John Brigham, a
state police officer who was assigned to the
district attorney's office, would also undoubtedly be getting into the act, for the state police
"cooperated" with local authorities in cases like
this one.

John Brigham was a cool professional of long
experience, with none of the human hangups
that sometimes arose to plague both Dr. Casey
and Chief Bert Higgins. Casey did not like the
thought of his questioning Clare.

Officer Sears said now, hesitantly, "We *will*
be talking to Miss Page, Mrs. Evans. But, just

for now, when did *you* last see Mr. Banning?''

"I don't know," Clare said, and even Carla raised her eyebrows.

Clare shook her head slightly, and her smile was bitter. "I really don't know," she said. "The precise moment, that is. I saw Gregory all afternoon and evening, except for the time when he was closeted in his studio with the Van Houdens. He *was* the host and he circulated. He and I met in passing; at the bar, refilling our drinks, or when we happened to stop to chat with the same group of people at the same time."

"Did he seem to be enjoying himself?" Sears asked.

"Very much so. When Greg gives a party he's master of the situation, and there's nothing Greg loves—*loved*—more than being the master of a situation." Momentarily, she was bleak. She said, "I can't believe he's dead."

"Neither can I," said Carla, and stared into a glass now empty. "I keep thinking that he's going to walk in here."

But she wouldn't want him to, Casey thought, and filed this thought in what seemed to be a growing file of disturbing ideas.

A voice came from the doorway, and Carla jumped visibly. Tony Mayo said, "Hi, may I join you?"

Carla said irritably, "Good God, you startled me!"

"Sorry," he said. "I came in the back way." He smiled across at Clare. "It's a Cape Cod custom," he told her.

"So I've gathered," she said.

Tony was wearing a bright yellow shirt and plaid slacks but despite his sartorial splendor he looked as tired as the rest of them. Dr. Casey suddenly realized that he had been up for thirty-odd hours, and felt it. So had Clare, for that matter; at least he doubted that she'd taken time out for any sleep. Carla had slept for a few hours because he had sedated her. Even John Sears, who had been on the midnight-to-eight shift, was working past his usual time.

He stood and said, "I've got to be getting along. Have you finished here, Sears?"

"Yes," said John Sears, but a bit unhappily, and so Casey asked the question for him.

"Tony," he said, "we've been trying to pinpoint the last time each of us saw Greg Banning. What about you?"

Tony Mayo frowned. "I don't know," he admitted, and a smile flitted across Clare's face. "That is, he was here, there and everywhere, if you know what I mean. Very much the genial host. I must have run into him a dozen times over the course of the party. He seemed to be having more fun than anybody, or maybe it was just the liquor. It surprised me, anyway."

"Why?"

"Because we'd been talking with Florence Page about those people from New York he had in the studio with him when we got here. I had the impression that getting their commission meant a lot, yet it evidently had fallen through. It seems as if Greg should have been upset about this."

A can of worms, Casey thought. You've opened up yet another can of worms, Tony, and how many will there be?

Carla said, almost hostilely, "The Van Houdens didn't mean that much. Greg had more clients than he could handle."

She was defending her late husband, and this, too, didn't fit the pattern, but Casey didn't pursue it.

"I'll talk to you later, Tony," he said, and Tony Mayo nodded.

Carla started to rise, to stretch her hands out to him; for a moment he was afraid she was going to plead with him to stay.

He said, before she could speak, "I'll be in touch, Carla," then nodded briefly to Clare, and made his way out of the room, with John Sears at his heels.

10

Dr. Casey's lawn furniture had seen better days. It had belonged to his Aunt Agatha and was fashioned of wicker, long ago painted white and now peeling in patches. He tried to remember to take the upholstered cushions indoors when rain threatened, almost always forgot to do so, and so now there were lumps. Chief Higgins, stretching out his long length, squirmed and said, "This might do for a Hindu fakir. It's not quite a bed of nails, but close to it!"

He accepted the tall glass of bourbon and water that Casey handed him, and sighed. "This," he said, "has been a hell of a Labor Day."

"You had plans?" Casey asked him, for Higgins was a widower like himself. Years ago, his pretty blond wife had died in childbirth, as had the son she was bearing him.

Higgins said, "I didn't have any plans, exactly. But I was thinking of parking the cruiser on top of one of the bridges over the Mid Cape and waving goodbye to them."

"Them" referred to the summer visitors who, today, were leaving Cape Cod by the thousands. Since the previous June, Higgins and his men had

coped with a burgeoning population that
strained their facilities, to say nothing of their
patience. Labor Day meant surcease.

"Been much of a traffic jam?" Casey asked,
and the chief nodded.

"Both bridges tied up. Traffic backed solid for
miles. Glad I don't work at *that* end of the Cape,"
referring to the territory from Hyannis to the
Cape Cod Canal.

Casey agreed, surveyed two of his wicker
chairs, and settled for what appeared to be the
lesser of two evils. Even so, he flinched as he sat
down, and the chief said, "Serves you right.
Look, they'll be having sales on summer furniture all through September."

"I'll try to get to one," Casey promised. He
sampled his drink and diagnosed it as good, very
good indeed.

It was late afternoon, just about the hour when
he had set out for the Bannings' party, the day
before. They were sitting at the rear of the
house, looking out upon Casey's back acreage
and the old, abandoned apple orchard that he
one day hoped to revitalize.

Higgins said, "Why did the Bannings decide to
try living here year-round? Do you know?"

"I suspect it was a question of money," Casey
replied. "At the party yesterday Florence Page
told Tony and me that Greg really needed that
big job from those New York people. It surprised
me. I suppose I took it for granted that Banning
was well heeled. I know he gets a mint when he
paints anything. But Florence pointed out that

he's been going commercial for years. He's been doing covers for some of the more popular magazines, but I'd thought nothing of it, to tell you the truth. Florence said, though, that he wouldn't have been doing them for any reason except money.''

"I went back there a couple of hours ago for the other Moses bottle and tried to talk to Carla Banning," Higgins said. "She was pretty well bombed. She hits the stuff hard, doesn't she?"

"Yes," Dr. Casey said reluctantly.

"Really an alcoholic?"

"Just about, unfortunately.''

"Her sister stayed right in the room like she was some sort of guardian," Higgins said. "I got the feeling she was afraid Carla was going to let something slip. I can't figure whether she's worried about Carla or herself. Know what I mean?"

"Yes.''

"Those two bottles," the chief went on, "From what I understand Banning bought at least one of them at some flea market and it was supposed to be old. Maybe they both are. You think Eleanor Chase would know?"

"I think she might.''

"Well, when I get them back from the lab we can ask her.''

The police cruiser was parked around the corner of the garage, out of sight of the road, as was Dr. Casey's yellow station wagon. The quiet was wonderful, and both men paused to enjoy it.

Then Higgins said, "Of course I had to call Brigham.''

"I assumed you would."

"I never like working with him," the chief admitted, "but what can I do? Fortunately, he was off the Cape for the holiday. I left a message. I said it could wait till tomorrow. That's why I went around to see some of these people this afternoon. Florence Page, Brent Nickerson, the Baileys. . . ."

Casey raised his eyebrows. "All of them?"

"Caught them at home," the chief said. "They were avoiding the traffic. I figured it might be that way."

He shifted position, trying to get comfortable. He said, "Talked to Mary Blodgett, too, but Bart Smith was out catering again, so I'll try to get to him tonight." He frowned. "I wish Carla Banning had kept a guest list. What was this, some last-minute idea?"

"More or less, I suppose," Dr. Casey said. "She called me Friday."

"Well, you'd think she would have kept some sort of list with a party that big. She promised she'd try to remember everyone who came, and her sister said she'd help, though she says she didn't know many of the people. I asked each person I talked to if they'd try to remember who they saw there, too, make a list and turn it over to me. I'm going to ask you to do the same thing."

Casey smiled faintly. "I can almost tell you right now," he said. "The Baileys, Florence Page, Tony, Brent Nickerson, Greg, of course, and Carla, and Clare Evans, and then there was

Greg's lawyer from New York—what's his name—Fawcett, I think.''

Higgins nodded, ''That's right. Robert Fawcett.''

''I · remember seeing that couple from New York, the Van Houdens, leaving the studio, but to tell you the truth, although I talked to a number of other people in passing, they're blurs as far as identity is concerned. Mostly Greg's friends. I'd know their faces if I were to see them again, but I can't put names to them.''

''That's what everyone says, even Carla herself,'' the chief complained. ''She says most of the people were friends of Greg's, and he called them himself.''

The chief finished his drink and put the glass down on the ground beside him. He said, ''One thing I found out: the association between Greg Banning and Hank Bailey and Florence Page goes way back. They all went to art school together in New York. Bailey says Banning was a bastard even then. He knew he was good, and I guess he was hard to take. He had that way with women, too. I got a strong feeling, talking to Florence Page, that she and Banning were pretty close for a time, back in those days.''

''Devon never fails to surprise me,'' Casey said. ''According to the local gossip, which I don't usually repeat, it was *Bailey* and Florence who had something going for a while.''

''I know,'' said the chief. ''I also know Jane Bailey was supposed to have had an affair with Banning a couple of summers ago. Maybe that's true, maybe it isn't, but what I'm talking about goes way back. Like twenty years back."

"And you think Greg Banning was Florence's lover?"

"I think so."

"Then that would give us the old hell-hath-no-fury routine," Casey observed. "Evidently Florence has managed to con the Van Houdens' business away from Greg and I wondered why she was so gleeful about it. I took it for granted it was a professional thing, but if you're right we've got passion entering the picture, too."

"Right, and that also goes for Bailey. He hated Banning's guts, and he doesn't make any bones about it."

"Well, Greg Banning didn't do much to make himself loved," Casey said dryly. "I've been aboard when he called Bailey a hack right to his face."

"Bailey *is* a hack and he knows it, which makes it even worse," the chief said. "I think Bailey is a guy who could use a shrink. He's full of hangups. And in his knowing that Banning, who's been one-upping him all his life professionally, was sleeping with his wife—"

"But that's been awhile," Dr. Casey protested.

"So sometimes it takes awhile," said Higgins. "Things can simmer a long time till they get to the boiling point or maybe Bailey just found out about it yesterday. That can happen, too."

Casey shook his head. "I don't think so," he said. "If I'm right, this was no impulse crime."

He finished his own drink. He said, "I hope there was enough in those two bottles for analysis."

"The one in the dining-room cupboard was nearly a quarter full," the chief said. "I asked Mary Blodgett about it and she said she took it herself from the outside bar to the cupboard where it was always kept."

He sighed. "Percy Blodgett's not in very good shape. He's in a wheelchair all the time now. He never did get over their daughter's death. Seemed to take it harder than Mary did; differently, at least."

"Did he ever go back to work after their daughter died?"

"I don't think so. He had his stroke not too long after. He was working for Fulcher's Hardware, had been for years. Fortunately they gave him a pension."

"Their daughter was killed in an accident, wasn't she?"

"Car crash," Higgins said. "About six, seven years ago—not too long before you came down. It was around this time of year. Evidently she'd been out with some summer guy, they'd been drinking. They were using her car—we figured she must have dropped him off and started home, and she crashed into a tree down in Eastham. She was killed instantly.

"Percy blamed the guy she was with who, of course, never came forward. Said he never should have let her drive. Mary, well, maybe she had more religion than Percy, or something. She seemed to accept it better. At least she kept going, but Percy gave up, that was the difference in them. Then, after he had his stroke, Mary had to keep going."

"She's a hard worker," Casey said.

"And then some," the chief agreed. "God, the woman's everywhere. She went home at noon, that's where I caught up with her, fixing Percy's lunch. Afterward, she was going over to work in Olson's Liquor Store for the afternoon. Incidentally, she says she thinks there must have been at least ninety or a hundred people at the party. For a while Bertha Murphy was out in the kitchen. Mary would ferry glasses out to her and Bertha'd wash 'em and Mary'd take them back out to the bar. Then Bertha had to leave, so Mary kept lugging and washing herself, trying to keep ahead. She went home and got Percy's supper around seven or so—just missed the commotion over Banning—then she came back later to help Bart clean up. . . ."

"I know. I talked to her."

"Yes, she said so. Well, she said she automatically put the Moses bottle back in its place, didn't think anything of it. I asked her, asked Bart, too, if anyone else ever drank that stuff, and they said no. I guess Banning never offered it to anyone else. It was sort of his private thing."

The chief looked at his watch and started to get up but Casey said, "Sit tight. I'll make us another."

"Well," Higgins hesitated, and then succumbed. "Okay."

Dr. Casey refilled the two glasses, found cheese

and crackers, and went back outside. He cut a substantial chunk of cheddar and handed it to the chief, then cut one for himself and asked, "How did Florence Page explain being in Banning's studio?"

"So," said Higgins, "Carla filled you in on that, did she?"

"She said it was Florence who told her Banning was sick."

"Yes. Well, Florence said he asked her to come over to the studio with him, he said he had something to show her.

"She was surprised at Banning's request, but she went with him because, as she put it, she didn't want to make a 'thing' out of it. When they got to the studio, though, he didn't have anything he wanted to show her; what he wanted was to talk about the Van Houden deal. She says he knew the Van Houdens had decided in her favor, and he asked if he could collaborate with her."

"That doesn't sound like Greg Banning!" Casey exclaimed.

"No, it doesn't, unless he really *was* strapped for money," the chief conceded. "I can get a better idea when I talk to his lawyer. Fawcett is staying at the Bayside Motel, and he'll be around till after the funeral."

"What did Florence say about collaborating?"

"She says she told Banning to go to hell, and I believe her. Then she says all of a sudden Banning's eyes looked peculiar, and he seemed to reel. He said to her, 'Christ, I'm going to be sick,'

and he made a rush for the bathroom and she
could hear him vomiting. After a couple of
minutes he came back, and she asked him if he
was okay, and he said, 'Just dizzy,' and poured
himself another drink. But he was very shaky, so
she decided to go and get Carla.''

Dr. Casey had been in the process of cutting off
another chunk of cheese. He paused, with the
knife in midair. He said, ''Banning poured himself another drink?''

''That's right.''

''From *what*?''

''From a green bottle that he kept in a cupboard,'' said the chief succinctly. And he nodded. ''Yes. Florence said it was shaped like an old
man with a long beard.''

11

AT FOUR O'CLOCK Tuesday morning the telephone next to Dr. Casey's bed rang, and he reached for it blindly, fighting his way out of sleep.

"Lon?" It was Carla. "Lon, you've got to come out here!"

He focused on his bedside clock, read the figures correctly, and groaned. He tried to be patient. "What is it, Carla?" he asked her.

"He's *here*," she said in a voice tinged with hysteria.

"Who?" Dr. Casey asked.

"Greg," she said. "Who else? He's *here*, Lon. I can hear him breathing." She started to sob. "Oh, *Jesus*!" she said.

"Carla," he said sharply. "Stop it! You've got to get a grip on yourself."

"Goddammit," said Carla, "don't treat me like a child, Lon. I tell you he's here! I can *feel* him!"

"Greg is dead," he said flatly.

Her laugh was high-pitched. "That's what you think! Greg will never be dead. He was too *mean* to die."

"Where's your sister?"

"Clare? Asleep." Again, that near-hysterical

laugh. "The sleep of the just. It isn't Clare that Greg wants. It's me."

"Are you in your room?"

"I'm in the living room," said Carla. "I can't go upstairs. Every time I try to go upstairs he goes up ahead of me. He waits for me just inside the bedroom door. If I try to go in there he'll *possess* me."

Dr. Casey said wearily, "Pour yourself another drink Carla. I'll be right down."

During the night the weather had finally fulfilled the promise of yesterday's lurid sunrise. Now rain slashed down and wind whipped the tops of the tall pines around the house in a kind of *danse macabre*. This, he knew, meant that it would be really wild on The Heights. Here on Fuller Road he was protected by trees planted by an earlier, farsighted owner, and they gave him a natural shield against the weather.

As he drove toward the ocean the storm seemed to rise to meet him; he could feel the sway of the car—must be gale-force winds, he thought. His windshield wipers worked furiously, and still couldn't keep pace with the rain.

He parked in the driveway at the back of the Banning house, made a run for the kitchen door, and was thankful to find it unlocked. Then he stood with his raincoat dripping on the brick-patterned floor, wishing that he had taken the long way around even if it meant getting wetter. Clare Evans was at the stove, heating something in a saucepan.

She turned toward him and said coldly, "I'm

sorry. I should have stayed in bed. I didn't know I would be interrupting a rendezvous."

He was normally slow to anger, but now he felt it flaring. He tossed down a verbal glove. He said, "Look—just why the hell *do* you have it in for me?"

She stared at him. She took the saucepan off the stove. Then she flared, too. "Because you've let my sister become a damned drunk."

"I?" He was truly startled.

"Yes. She's in love with you, any damned fool can see that, but you've just let her go on and on—"

"*Let* her?" He laughed shortly. "Come off it, Clare. You know I haven't had a damned thing to do with it. We've been over that before."

"Regardless of what you say she is your patient, isn't she?"

"To a point," he conceded. "She's consulted me for a couple of sore throats, some minor aches and pains. She's been strictly a summer patient till now, remember? I presumed she had a doctor in New York. And, to tell you the truth, although naturally I took care of her when she called, I didn't encourage the calls. I can do without someone else's wife drumming up that sort of a—fixation."

"Now she's a widow," Clare said briefly.

"A very recent widow," Casey pointed out. "The same thing still holds. I can do without someone else's widow drumming up that kind of a fixation."

"So you'd rather simply let her drink herself to death?"

"That's none of my business," he said.

"Then you're a hell of a doctor," Clare told him.

He smiled wryly. He said, "Being a doctor doesn't give a person the right to invade someone else's life. Carla's drinking *is* none of my business—unless she approaches me about it. The problem wasn't all that bad the summer before this, but more recently I have tried to get a message across and she hasn't listened. She doesn't want to listen. I might add, in case you don't know it, that a doctor has very little chance with an alcoholic who insists on turning the subject off."

"So you consider Carla an alcoholic?"

"Yes."

"At least you're honest," she admitted.

He divested himself of his raincoat and hung it over a chair to dry. He said, "I'll pass up that one. Now, where is Carla? Does she still think Greg is breathing down her neck?"

It was Clare's turn to be startled. "She's in the living room and I'd say she's nearly bombed out, but she hasn't mentioned Greg. What gave you that idea?"

"She called me," he said. "At 4:00 A.M., I might add. This is no rendezvous, Mrs. Evans. It is just a response to terror, hysteria, whatever you want to call it."

He left her with that, picking up his black medical bag and taking it with him.

He sensed that she was following him but he didn't look to make sure, and the sound of footsteps was lost in the thickness of the diningroom rug. In any case he was annoyed at her. In the kitchen he had had a nearly uncontrollable desire to take her by the shoulders and shake her thoroughly. He decided that, in her way, she was as bad as her sister.

Carla had curled up in the corner of the livingroom couch and was asleep; her empty glass stood on the coffee table. She looked pale, fragile, like a weary child, and Dr. Casey stared down at her feeling helpless, and decidedly frustrated.

He turned, and as he suspected, Clare had come into the room behind him. He motioned for silence, then made a noiseless exit. In the dining room he said to Clare, "There's no sense in waking her up now. She may sleep like that for hours. If she doesn't, I'm going to give you something that will dull the edges for her. Sedatives and alcohol don't mix very well, but this will be safe."

They went back to the kitchen and he sat down at the table, took pills out of his bag, got out his prescription pad.

"I've got enough here to go through today," he told Clare, "but I'd suggest you get this prescription filled later. Try to get her to take one of these every four hours until after the funeral. It should be just enough to calm her down."

Clare was wearing a pale yellow robe. She took the vial of pills and put it in a pocket. She was watching him narrowly and she said, "Just what did you mean about Carla thinking that Greg was breathing down her neck?"

"Hallucination," he said briefly.

Clare nodded. "She really *has* been pushing it," she said. "I don't think all this really hit her until Tony Mayo started talking about the arrangements. Of course she started drinking as soon as she came out from under the sedative you gave her last night."

Clare frowned, and it was a painful expression. She said, "I didn't realize until recently that she was so much into it. Not just drinking, either."

"What else?"

"Drugs. A variety of them. Greg was a great experimenter, and Carla was gullible enough to go along with him." She looked across at him. "Greg was a very selfish man," she said flatly.

She turned to the saucepan she had been working over when he first came in. "I couldn't sleep, so I came down to make some cocoa," she confessed. "Would you like some?"

It was years since he'd had cocoa. He said, surprised at her asking him, "Yes, please. I would."

She got out cups and saucers, turned the stove back on, reheated, stirred. She filled the cups and brought the cocoa across to him, then sat down on the other side of the table.

Again she looked at him narrowly and she said, "You're bushed, aren't you?"

"Tired, yes. But I imagine you are, too."

"Dr. Casey," Clare said, "I'm sorry."

"Why?"

The blue eyes were direct. "You haven't deserved some of the things I've said to you, or my attitude toward you in general. I realize you can't force Carla to stop drinking. It was just wishful thinking on my part. Evidently there's not much I can do about it, either. She is older than I am, as she'd be the first to point out. I've always been put in the baby-sister role."

She hesitated, then asked, "Do you suppose once the funeral is over we could persuade her to try A.A.?"

"I don't know," he said honestly. "A person has to be self-motivated. When is the funeral?"

"Wednesday," said Clare. "Tomorrow, that is. It's a memorial service, really. Greg specified cremation. He left a paper in his studio. Carla knew about it. It's just a simple statement, detailing his wishes. I was surprised by it. I would have imagined Greg thought himself pretty immortal."

Dr. Casey took a chance. "Why did you dislike him so?" he asked.

She didn't hedge. "Because of the things he did to people," she said frankly. "Because of the way he robbed them of their self-respect, without giving a damn. I've seen it so often. Years ago in New York, when I was at art school and he was my teacher I would watch him cut someone down mercilessly, without a qualm. It was as if diminishing someone else bolstered his own ego, as if he needed this, and I never did understand why. He was a very talented artist, very much in demand—at least until the last couple of years."

"What do you mean by that?"

"Well, Greg had been slipping," she said. "Drugs, drink, too much sex—they all began to take their toll. His hands weren't as steady as they used to be, nor his visual perception as good, and it began to show in his work. If you look at some of his more recent things and compare, you'll see what I mean. You can see the deterioration."

She sighed. "There was still a lot to learn from him, though," she said. "That's why I could forget what a bastard he was and go walking with him, both of us with our sketch pads. He could make everything around you come alive, he was an entirely different person at such moments. You could even see what it was about him that made women fall in love with him."

He looked at her sharply, and she shook her head. "No, doctor," she said, "I wasn't in love with Greg; I never had an affair with him, even though I know Carla has had her suspicions. Life's complicated enough without adding something like that, don't you think? I introduced Carla to him, you know, and she introduced me to Harry Evans. We both got married, and we both made mistakes."

He looked his question, and she said briefly, "It wasn't a good marriage, doctor, not any better than Carla's. Oh, it was exciting for a time, but with Harrison Evans life was a continual public-relations campaign. We were talking divorce when he was killed.

"On the other hand, I think Carla would have

stayed with Greg. Maybe, in a way, she deserved him. I love Carla, but I realize she's a selfish person, too. Even so, I'd do anything for her. . . ."

Even cover up murder, he wondered, remembering the Moses bottle. Or, perhaps, even commit murder yourself?

He finished the cocoa and glanced at his watch. "Five o'clock," he said. "Maybe if we're both lucky we can get a couple of hours sleep."

"Maybe," she agreed. "You can hear the surf pounding from my bedroom window. I love it, but it keeps me awake. I guess I'm used to city sounds."

She went to the door with him. The wind howled around the corners of the house, a banshee that moaned one moment and shrieked the next. The rain had become a waterfall, slithering down in sheets. By daylight the ocean would be whipped to a full fury, the cresting breakers plume-sprayed; white horses, the local people called them.

Clare shivered. "What a night!" she said. "I'm sorry Carla called you out in it, and all for nothing, too."

He looked down at her. "I wouldn't say that," he told her gently.

12

Gregory Banning's memorial service brought people in the art world to Devon from New York, California, Chicago, and various other points, plus an outpouring of the local population who attended from a frankly acknowledged sense of curiosity.

The Parkington Funeral Home was taxed to capacity and beyond. Tony Mayo, accustomed to having organizations borrow chairs from him for their different functions, was forced to send his men out to scout for chairs from others. The result still was standing room only for quite a few.

Carla, dressed entirely in white, made such a poignant figure that the picture taken of her on the steps of the funeral home after the service by an ambitious local news photographer was sent out over the wire service and made front page the next day in papers across the country.

A selected few had been invited to come back to the house after the service, Dr. Casey among them, but he excused himself, pleading the need to visit a patient at the hospital in Hyannis.

This was not entirely untrue; he did go and visit the patient, but to keep his own word rather than from a sense of any urgency.

Wednesday, actually, was supposed to be his day off, the day when the phone went on answering service and he strove to be incommunicado, and on rare occasions even succeeded.

He had not gone back to the Banning house again the day before claiming that bit of extra sleep he had mentioned to Clare first, then making house calls, holding office hours, and in the evening, going to the weekly dinner of the Conference Club, a civic-fraternal organization indigenous to the Commonwealth of Massachusetts.

The dinners were held at the Surf and Sand Club, a former whaling captain's home, now a popular dining place. Tony Mayo was also a club member, and they had managed a brief conversation in the bar over a post-dinner drink.

Tony had said Carla had been quite composed in making the memorial service arrangements; for that matter, Banning had written down what he wanted, she had concurred, so there had been relatively little to discuss. There was the cost, of course, but she had given him the impression that money was no object. Later, however, Clare had gone to the door with him and had asked him to try to economize. Clare had told him that Carla didn't seem to realize there might not be much left.

Tony had already talked to Bert Higgins about

his impressions of the party and of Greg Banning's behavior, and had given him a list of the guests he could remember. Greg had seemed to him, as he evidently had to everyone else, to be riding high, elated, feeling his drinks but enjoying every minute. Thinking back, Tony had remembered seeing Jane Bailey and Greg go into the studio together, at some point, but he had no idea of how long they had stayed there.

Wednesday morning Bert Higgins stopped by Casey's house to say that he had been talking to both Barton Smith and Mary Blodgett. Neither of them had been aware of the existence of a second Moses bottle.

The chief was not happy about the course of the investigation. "Hope the lab doesn't take too long getting those damned bottles back," he grumbled, and as it happened, the lab didn't.

Thursday morning at approximately seven o'clock, Chief Higgins's telephone call woke Dr. Casey up.

He had been dreaming that he was wandering, alone, through rooms of incredible Moorish architecture, looking for someone who managed to elude him at every turning. He would see a wisp of color, vanishing around a corner and he would be in pursuit once more, but, always, she would be gone.

He had almost caught up with her—or at least so he decided later—when the phone rang and the chief said accusingly, "You still in bed?"

"I was in the Alhambra," Casey said succinct-

ly, having recognized the edifice in his dreams
for what it was.

"You were where?"

"Actually," said Casey, "I've never been
there, but this makes me think I want to go."

There was an edge of alarm to the chief's voice.
"You all right, Pete?"

"Yes," said Casey. "I was asleep. You woke me
up."

"Oh," said the chief. "Well." Then, "I got the
lab report. Got it yesterday not long after I was at
your place and I tried to reach you, but all I could
get was your answering service."

"I went to Hyannis," said Dr. Casey, and much
as he liked Bert Higgins he felt faintly annoyed,
because it seemed as if he were forever explain-
ing even the slightest departure. "I went to a
movie at the mall and wasted my money. It was a
very bad movie."

I think, he told himself, maybe I *will* go to
Spain. He said to Bert Higgins, "What did they
find out?"

"Nothing from the bottles," said Bert Higgins.
"No evidence of any poison, that is, in either of
them. The one in the dining room had plenty in it
as you know. The other one, the one Mrs. Evans
was trying to hide, was empty. My guess would
be that she poured what was in it out into the
sand, but there were still dregs. They analyzed
zilch, as far as poison is concerned. However. . . ."

"Yes?"

"Banning was still alive when they got him to

the hospital last Sunday night and they pumped out his stomach, remember?''

"Right," said Casey. "That's basic treatment, under such circumstances."

"Well, since you evidently requested it, they saved the contents of the stomach and turned them over for analysis, and we've got the results on that, too."

"Yes?"

"It was methyl alcohol," Bert Higgins said.

SOMETIMES WHEN HE WAS REQUIRED to take up his role as a medical examiner Dr. Casey began to feel more like a juggler than a doctor.

It became a matter of trying to keep a balance between his practice on the one hand and working with the police on the other, and this was seldom easy.

Thursday was no exception. When Bert Higgins asked him to be at police headquarters at 1:00 P.M. to go over the Banning case, there seemed no alternative to postponing his afternoon office hours and putting a sign on the door to that effect. This he did, not without imagining, vividly, the reaction it would provoke in some of his patients.

He arrived at the police station ten minutes early and found Bert Higgins at his desk, surveying a miscellany of papers spread in front of him.

The chief said, "The lab has turned the bottles back to me. How about if we get Eleanor Chase to look at them this evening?"

"I think she'd be glad to."

1. How do you rate _____ ?
   (Please print book TITLE)

   (Please check (√) the appropriate box.)
   □ excellent   □ good   □ not so good
   □ very good   □ fair   □ poor

2. How likely are you to purchase another book in this series?
   □ definitely would purchase   □ definitely would not purchase
   □ probably would purchase   □ probably would not purchase

3. How do you compare this title with similar books you usually read?
   □ far better than others   □ not as good
   □ better than others   □ definitely not as good
   □ about the same

4. Have you any additional comments about this book?

   _____

   _____

5. How did you first become aware of this book?
   □ in-store display   □ talk show
   □ radio   □ read other titles
   □ magazine _____   □ other _____
                  (name)   (please specify)

6. What most prompted you to buy this book?
   □ title   □ picture on cover   □ back-cover story outline
   □ price   □ friend's recommendation □ read a few pages
   □ author   □ product advertising   □ other _____
                                                  (please specify)

7. How do you usually obtain your books?
   □ bookstore   □ department/discount store   □ subscription
   □ drugstore   □ convenience store   □ other
   □ borrow   □ supermarket   _____
                                                  (please specify)

8. What type(s) of paperback fiction have you purchased in the past
   3 months? Approximately how many?

                        No. purchased   No. purchased
   □ contemporary romance _____   □ western   _____
   □ historical romance   _____   □ contemporary novels _____
   □ gothic romance   _____   □ historical novels   _____
   □ romantic suspense   _____   □ science fiction/fantasy _____
   □ mystery/private eye _____   □ occult   _____
   □ action/adventure   _____   □ other   _____
   □ espionage   _____   _____
                                             (please specify)

9. Please indicate your age group and sex.   □ Male   □ Female
   □ younger than 15   □ 18-24   □ 35-49   □ 65 or older
   □ 15-17   □ 25-34   □ 50-64

Thank you for completing and returning this questionnaire.

Printed in Canada

NAME _____
ADDRESS _____
(Please Print)
CITY _____
ZIP CODE _____

"Another thing, Pete, Fawcett—Banning's lawyer—stayed over after the funeral so he could have a talk with Carla this morning. I told him I want to talk to him, too, and he seemed agreeable enough. I said it could be out at the Bannings or here, and he said he'd prefer here, so he's coming by around four. Think you could manage to drop in?"

Doctor Casey hesitated. "Bert. . . I *do* have a practice," he pointed out.

"Yeah, I know, but I don't have a murder every day of the week, thank God. Fawcett ought to be able to give us the facts about Banning's finances. In fact, it seems to me he ought to be able to shed some light on a number of things. I'd kind of like to have you around."

"I'll do my best."

"As to these damned bottles," the chief continued, "we know Banning was drinking from at least one of them, the one Bart Smith was using, but there's not a trace of methyl alcohol. How do you figure it?"

Dr. Casey was looking through the wide, front window that gave a view of the small, flag-centered crescent in front of the police station. He saw a state police car pull into the driveway then head toward the official parking lot at the side of the building.

"Brigham's arriving," he told Higgins, then said, "The bottles? I don't know, Bert. I think the methyl alcohol must have been mixed up with gin and *cassis* in *some* kind of container that Banning used more than once because the effect on him, over the course of the evening, was such a classic buildup."

He paused, "Maybe," he told Bert Higgins, "you should keep on looking. Maybe there's still another bearded prophet hanging around somewhere!"

13

Lieutenant John Brigham of the state police
was an efficient and respected man, but he was
not likable.

He had been assigned to the area district attorney's office for nearly four years, and so had
represented that arm of the law during Dr.
Casey's entire tenure as a medical examiner.

Brigham hailed from the Boston area. He was a
university graduate who had aspired toward law,
but for reasons that were never discussed had
made the state police a career instead.

He was a handsome man with finely chiseled
features and naturally wavy hair that had
silvered prematurely. He emphasized it by often
wearing gray, as he was today, and the effect
was glacial.

Taking turns Higgins and Casey filled Brigham
in on the details surrounding Gregory Banning's
death, and when they came to the story of the
Moses bottles, the state police lieutenant raised a
skeptical eyebrow.

"You say there are *three* of them?" he asked
Dr. Casey.

"No," Casey said, determined not to be put on

the defensive. "I'm only suggesting that there might be."

"What about you, Bert?" He turned to Chief Higgins. "Have you talked to the people who were at the party?"

"Officer John Sears, who is a bright boy, has been assigned to this investigation," Higgins said. "Either he's talked to them or I have, yes."

"But you say that there were nearly a hundred people at this shindig and you're narrowing down your interrogation principally to the local people you know. Don't you think that's limiting things too much?"

Bert Higgins *did* become defensive. "Carla Banning didn't keep a guest list," he said. "Lots of the people who were there have already gone back to New York or Boston or wherever they came from."

"Which makes it good procedure for you to concentrate on a handful? I don't buy that," Brigham said bluntly. "After all, Bert, the murderer didn't even have to be at the scene of the crime at the time of death. He could have been long gone when Banning collapsed."

"Not necessarily," Dr. Casey said.

"Why not?"

"Well, it's simple psychology, if you like," Casey said, feeling his way. "My personal feeling is that the person who killed Banning would have wanted to be around when he collapsed, to be sure his plan had worked. There was also a danger that someone else might have drunk some of Banning's brew.''

"If they had," Brigham said, "do you think the murderer would have come forward and announced it was poison?''

"Hardly. But there is the chance that the murderer might have been keeping an eye on things during the entire party. That he—or she—might have been able to forestall someone else taking a drink of the gin and *cassis*. Of course we don't know whether the poison was served at the bar or in the studio.''

"Or somewhere else?''

"I wouldn't think it was anywhere else, would you, Bert? This is only theory, of course, but my feeling is that Banning had two bottles. He kept one in his own studio and the other in the dining-room cabinet. It seems unlikely that he would have stocked a third area.''

"What are you trying to say?" Brigham demanded. "That the murderer brought one of these Moses bottles to the party himself, full of methyl alcohol and gin and that other stuff Banning drank, and then exchanged it for either the bar bottle or the bottle in the studio?''

"I think it's likely," Dr. Casey admitted.

Brigham's smile was thin. "Wouldn't this person have to have been quite a sleight-of-hand artist?''

"Not necessarily. As we've already said, it was a large party, lots of people milling around, noise, a certain amount of confusion. I do doubt that the bar played a part in this, though. Bart Smith was there himself most of the time, a couple of times when he went back into the house he had Mary Blodgett pinch-hit. It would have been difficult to make a substitution right in front of either of them and the bar was doing a steady business anyway; someone would surely have noticed a switch like that.

"No, I think the substitution was made in the studio. If, by chance, Greg Banning hadn't got around to drinking the methyl alcohol at the party he almost surely would have yesterday, or today, or tomorrow."

"Aren't you contradicting yourself?" Brigham asked. "You just said you thought the murderer wanted to be around when Banning collapsed."

"Yes, definitely, if the collapse took place at the party," Dr. Casey said. "But if Banning hadn't collapsed by the time the party was over, it wouldn't have made too much difference. I mean by that, it's unlikely anyone else would have been endangered. Neither Carla nor her sister would touch the gin and *cassis*, as I understand it, and most of the time Gregory Banning's studio was off limits anyway. He liked his privacy, and he had no objection to drinking alone."

The rest of the session with Brigham dealt with routine police business. Dr. Casey receded, and let Brigham and Higgins discuss procedure. Basically, this was Bert Higgins's case; the murder *had* taken place in Devon. But it was customary for the state police to step in to assist when even possible homicide was involved, and in reality Brigham was acting as an adjunct of the district attorney's office. If—when—Gregory Banning's murderer was found, it would be Brigham who would assist with the prosecution.

Finally Brigham left, and Casey drove back to his office to find patients literally waiting on the threshold. It was difficult to break away, and it was nearly a quarter-past four before he could get back to the police station.

Robert Fawcett was there, trying to conceal his impatience and doing a poor job of it. But, with Dr. Casey's appearance, Bert Higgins got down to essentials. Principally, he wanted to know the true story regarding Banning's financial affairs, and his decision to live year-round on the Cape.

Fawcett hesitated, frowned, and said, "I don't know about this, Chief. We're dealing with a lawyer-client relationship here, and there is such a thing as confidentiality."

"Banning is dead," Bert Higgins said.

"True," Fawcett admitted.

"Also," the chief said levelly, "Banning was murdered. That seems a good enough reason to me for you to tell me what I want to know."

Fawcett looked unhappy. He said, "Carla told me that you were working on a *supposition* of murder."

The chief glanced across at Casey, and he said quietly, "It isn't a supposition, Mr. Fawcett. Gregory Banning died of methyl alcohol poisoning."

"Methyl alcohol?" Fawcett asked. "Is that the stuff they used to call wood alcohol?"

Dr. Casey nodded. "Yes, though it is manufactured synthetically today. Back in the bootleg days, when so many people went blind or died from drinking it, it was distilled from wood, hence the name. Either variety is equally lethal."

"Where would anyone *get* something like that?"

"There are a number of possible sources. It isn't as easy to obtain as it used to be. Because it *is* such a violent poison, its use has been restricted. But it is still used in the manufacture of resins, dyes, drugs, perfume, making formaldehyde, even in automotive antifreezes. As I say, it *is* available."

Fawcett lighted a cigarette, and exhaled deeply. "Christ, what a mind!" he exclaimed.

Dr. Casey glanced up, surprised. "Mine?" he asked.

"No. Whoever did such a fiendish thing to Greg. They must have schemed, waited for the first opportunity—"

"Exactly," Casey agreed. "Banning was murdered by someone who gave it a lot of thought and was willing to wait for the right opportunity. That's why the chief says there is more than enough reason to talk about his affairs."

"I suppose you're right," the lawyer conceded. "Okay, then—Banning was on thin ice, financially. Years ago, long before I ever knew him, he started on an ego trip, and he never got to the end of it. He could be a hard man to take, then he would suddenly turn on the charm and make you feel you should do anything he wanted you to do.

"That sort of thing doesn't go over in business, though, and art, today, *is* business. For instance, Banning liked to stall. If he had a commission to do a magazine cover he was apt to make them sweat it out until the last minute. Or someone would commission him to do a portrait, and he might show up or he might not, depending on his mood. People got fed up with this kind of an attitude after a while.

"Eventually, Banning's own life-style began to take its toll. Liquor, drugs, women. He had a strong system, but it started to wear down and his work became affected. Banning hasn't finished a commission for the past two years."

Fawcett snuffed out his cigarette. "What I'm saying is that he hasn't made any money for the past two years," he told them. "It's been a juggling contest, liquidating an asset to catch up on a bill before his credit hit bottom."

"Is that why he decided to move to the Cape year-round?" Higgins asked.

Fawcett shook his head. "Not exactly. Banning couldn't really believe that he was going broke, or that he was losing his touch as an artist, so he started to blame everything on the city. He said each summer he became a new man, revitalized, ready to paint, just about the time Labor Day rolled around and he had to go back. He told me this year he wanted to stay on and paint on the

Cape off-season, to renew himself. Christ, he had
a thousand phrases.

"I was delighted. It meant that I could put the
New York studio in the hands of a real-estate
agent who could tout it as Banning's and get a big
price for it, and that's precisely what I did. The
studio is rented, which means we can all breathe
a little until Banning's estate is settled. Otherwise Carla might have had to go to work if she
wanted to drink regularly!"

14

ELEANOR CHASE HAD BEEN in an automobile accident the year before Dr. Casey moved to Cape Cod. She had walked with a cane ever since and was in pain almost constantly, but she was unfailingly cheerful, never complained, and kept busy. Dr. Casey, who inevitably acquired his share of hypochondriacs in the course of a work week, admired her tremendously.

Now he and Chief Higgins stood at her dining-room table, and the chief carefully unwrapped the two Moses bottles and put them in front of her.

Eleanor smiled. "Moses at the Spring, indeed," she said.

The chief was watching her narrowly. "Which of them?" he asked.

"Both of them," Eleanor said equably.

Bert Higgins frowned. "What I want to know, Mrs. Chase," he explained patiently, "is which one of them is a fake and which one is genuine? Can you tell?"

"Not necessarily," Eleanor said sweetly, and Dr. Casey couldn't resist a smile.

Paul Chase groaned, and looked at his wife

despairingly. ''Come *on*, Nell,'' he pleaded, ''the chief is going to have apoplexy.''

''There's no need to, Bert,'' Eleanor said cheerfully. ''I'm not an authority, mind you, and there might be some so-called antique experts who would differ with me, but the fact is that there are at least thirty varieties of the Moses at the Spring bottle. The first was put out by the company in Poland Springs, Maine in 1876; there were at least three more versions prior to World War I and a considerable number since. In the thirties they were even putting gin in bottles like this one. I would think any of the earlier versions would be considered ''original'' at this point because now there are reproductions on the market. In the past few years they've been reproducing just about everything.''

''So,'' said the chief, ''what you're telling me is that there's no way of saying which of these two was the bottle Greg Banning bought himself at a flea market?''

''Yes,'' Eleanor admitted regretfully, ''I suppose that *is* what I'm telling you, though the one on the left is probably a bit older than the one on the right.''

''What might he have paid for either one of them—just as a matter of interest?''

''A few dollars.''

''Under twenty-five?''

''I should think so, yes.''

''Suppose I wanted to go buy one of these bottles? Would it be difficult to find one?''

''Dr. Casey could give you one if he were so inclined," Eleanor pointed out. "You did say there's one in the cupboard off your dining room, didn't you, Lon?"

"Yes. I checked."

The chief frowned. "Suppose I didn't know Dr. Casey. Would it be hard to come across one?"

"You could get a reproduction in a gift shop, and heaven knows we have our choice of gift shops here on the Cape," Eleanor said. "For that matter, there was quite a nice older bottle in the Community Exchange in Orleans last summer. I think it was priced at twelve dollars. They're not a drug on the market, certainly, but they're not all that rare, either."

"Well," said the chief, and rewrapped his bottles, "thank you."

Eleanor's alert, hazel eyes were sympathetic. "I'm afraid I've confused you more than helped you, Bert."

"No," Bert Higgins shook his head. "Disappointed me, maybe."

"I'm sorry."

"Not your fault," he told her.

"How about some coffee? Or Paul can fix you both a drink."

"Rain check?" the chief asked.

"Certainly," she assured him, "You, too, Lon?"

"Yes. I'd better run along with Bert."

She followed them to the door, leaning on her cane. She said, "I can hardly wait till you decide to clean that cupboard out, Alonzo."

"When you do," Paul Chase cautioned, "be sure she's the last to know about it!"

THE CHIEF PARKED the police cruiser back of Dr. Casey's house, and as the two men walked down the driveway Higgins said, "Bad luck about the Moses bottles. I expected them to be a hell of a lot rarer."

"Find the bottle, find the killer?" Casey suggested.

"Not quite, but I thought it would be a lead. This way, it could almost be a Coke bottle, though I'll admit Moses had more class."

Higgins sighed. "Anyway, I'm sure you're right, of course."

"About what?"

"About there being a third Moses bottle. *The* bottle. I doubt if we'll ever find it. Where do you suppose it is, Pete?"

"Smashed, I should imagine. Maybe with a lot of trash in the town dump or at the bottom of some inlet or pond, weighted down so it won't float to shore. It's a cinch it's someplace where we're not apt to come across it."

Bert Higgins frowned. "I keep wondering why she was so damned anxious to hide it when it wasn't even the right bottle," he mused.

Clare, running down the steps at dawn, groveling in the sand, covering her tracks so that, but for a stroke of luck, the bottle would still be hidden along the face of the sandy cliffs beneath the Banning house.

Why, indeed?

IT WAS NINE O'CLOCK when the chief left. Dr.
Casey turned on the TV in the library, switched
channels, found nothing to capture his interest
and so turned it off again.

The old house seemed gloomy tonight—there
was a kind of spiritual dustiness about it. It occurred to him that it hadn't been a home for a
long, long time. A home connoted warmth, com-
panionship, love. During Agatha's long, solitary
tenure the house had had none of these things.

Yet, he told himself, these walls must have wit-
nessed every possible emotion, the ultimates in
joy and tragedy, weddings and births and deaths,
the gamut run not once but many times over a
space of decades.

In the big four-poster bed he now occupied,
men and women must once have found each
other, yet now there was a sterility to the bed,
too, a dryness, like the rustle of a withered leaf.

He was too *young* to live in an atmosphere like
this, he told himself, then stopped, astonished.
He could not remember when he last had coupled
youth and himself in the same thought.

He kept a decanter of brandy on a side table in
the library and now he splashed some into a
snifter, surprised to find that his hand was
trembling slightly. The crystal facets of the
decanter winked back at him and he was reminded of Greg Banning, who undoubtedly had
poured his last drink in much this same manner,
only from a Moses bottle, not a crystal decanter.

He finished the brandy, and was trying to
decide whether to try TV again or to start a new

old book when the doorbell rang. For a moment, a surprisingly giddy moment, he wondered if it might possibly be Clare. But it wasn't Clare. It was Florence Page.

Her pleated dress was a whirl of astonishing colors. She had flung a lacy sweater around her shoulders, and with her dark, shoulder-length hair and expert makeup she looked, at first, like a very glamorous and expensive lady.

Then one came to her eyes, and paused to read a horror story.

She said abruptly, "I know I'm intruding. No—" as he protested "—don't be polite, doctor. I *intend* to intrude."

He stood aside to let her in, and she said, "Where can we talk?"

"Well," he said, "I was in the library."

He led the way and she, following, said, "The house seemed so dark. You weren't asleep?"

"No."

"Do you live here by yourself? No house-keeper?"

"Just a part-time one."

"I remember your aunt," Florence Page said. "She came to an art show we had once on the Village Green. She was quite formidable."

"Yes, she was," he conceded.

They had reached the library. They stood in the middle of the room, seemingly out of conversation. Then she said, her voice breaking on a sob, "Oh, Christ! Help me, will you?"

He poured brandy for her without being asked, and she took the snifter and drank. She sat down

in a maroon armchair that immediately went to
war with several of the shades in her dress and
said, "Oh, dear God! You must think I am an
idiot!"

"No," he protested. "Not at all!"

The horror story still lingered in her eyes, but
temporarily was veiled by a touch of amusement.
She said, "Well, I *am* an idiot. But I had to come.
Perhaps what I'm going to ask you is confiden-
tial, I don't know, and I realize that you don't
know me very well; we've just met at Greg's a
few times. But I don't know Chief Higgins, or any
of the other officials at all. So. . . ."

"Yes?"

She leaned forward, the haunted eyes fixed on
his face. She said, "Everyone's talking murder.
But isn't there a chance, a good chance, that
Greg could have committed suicide?"

15

DR. CASEY, PAINFULLY AWARE of her intensity, hedged.

He said, "Miss Page. We're still waiting for reports from the state pathologist's office in Boston, and it takes a while. Nothing will be official until we get them."

She came straight to the point. "There's a full-scale investigation going on while you're waiting, isn't there?"

"Miss Page—" he began, but she interrupted him.

"Call me Florence," she said, then added, "what I want to know—what I *have* to know—is whether this investigation is into Greg's murder or his suicide?"

He looked across at her. "Okay, then, Florence," he said levelly. "Why do you have to know?"

Her lips twisted in a surprisingly poignant smile. She said, "Nothing comes cheap, does it."

"Is that a question or a statement?"

"A statement. I answered the question myself a long time ago." She paused, then said thoughtfully, "Talking to a doctor is almost like talking to a priest, isn't it?"

He smiled. "I don't think of it that way," he admitted. "I don't consider this a confessional."

"I can appreciate that. But, you would maintain confidentiality, wouldn't you?"

"Look," he said, "I don't want to make an issue out of this, but you're not my patient, you know."

"No doctor-patient relationship?"

"That's right."

"Then I shall have to rely upon your honor," she said. "And God knows that's a strange enough word for me to use, let alone to count on."

"Please," he said. "I think you know I'm not about to go out and shout anything you might tell me, but if it's something important in connection with Greg Banning's death the police should know about it, and I have an allegiance to them, too."

"It isn't," she said. "It's important to me, that's all. More than important. It's vital."

He said patiently, "You're leaving me behind."

"It's a matter of insurance," she said bluntly. "If Greg was murdered, the insurance will pay off. If he committed suicide, it won't."

He frowned. "*You* had insurance on Gregory Banning's life?"

"Not for myself, for our daughter."

The word became a small crystal pendant suspended between them. Florence Page said, not without a touch of maliciousness, "Well, that finally grabbed you, didn't it?"

She sat back and let the amusement take over, for just a moment. She said, "You've a rather sleepy way of looking at people when you're trying to make them do the talking, doctor. It's artful. Almost tranquillizing. But just now your eyes opened wide, wide, wide."

He smiled ruefully. "Do you blame me?" he asked.

"No."

"You did say *daughter*?"

"Yes."

"And you said *our* daughter."

"Yes. Greg's and mine. She's twenty-two and hopelessly retarded. She's been in an institution—a private institution—all her life. It takes a mint to pay for it."

She swallowed hard and asked, abruptly, "Do you have a cigarette?"

"No, I'm sorry. I stick to pipes." Then, remembering, "Wait, I think someone *did* leave a partial pack here a couple of weeks ago, but they'd be pretty stale."

"It doesn't matter."

He found the cigarettes and lighted one for her. She looked at her own trembling fingers and said, "God, I *am* a nervous wreck."

"Florence," Dr. Casey said slowly, "this is a police matter, this business of Greg Banning's death. I'm not at all sure that you should be talking to me, and I mean this for your own sake."

She looked at him narrowly. She said, "That sounds like murder."

"I didn't say that."

Unexpectedly she smiled. "Don't you see," she told him, "I want it to be murder. If Greg had to die violently I'd much prefer murder to suicide. The past couple of years have been bad enough. I've had to extract the monthly payments from him." She grimaced. "Like getting blood. Now, well, without the policy I couldn't possibly afford to keep Lisa in the school she's in. That's what they call it. A school. She'd have to go to some horrible state place where they might be cruel to her."

"Florence," he said, "you're pushing a needless panic button." He hesitated, then he said, his voice gentle, "Tell me about Lisa."

She shrugged. "What is there to tell? She happened, that's all. Greg and I were in art school, we lived together in a little place in the Village. I got pregnant, and I had this weird streak of morality. Also, I loved him. I wanted his child.

"He walked out and left me to handle it on my own. He found someone older and richer. I stayed and had Lisa, and if she had been normal I would have built my life around her. But, she wasn't normal.

"I would never have sought Greg out again for myself, but Lisa was as much his as she was mine. So, when Lisa was a few weeks old I followed Greg up here to the Cape. He was in Chatham with his rich benefactor; she had a place overlooking Pleasant Bay."

"You knew her?"

"I knew who she was," Florence said. "You would, too, if I mentioned her name, but there's no need for that. She and Greg broke up years ago.

"Anyway, I didn't waste time trying to write Greg or phone him. I knew he would only brush me off. I rented a car and drove to Chatham and I remember I drove back and forth in front of her house a couple of times until I got up enough courage to face them.

"I parked right in front of the door, and as I walked across the lawn I heard voices. Sure enough, they were around at the rear of the house having drinks on the patio.

"I'll never forget the look on Greg's face. It was classic. She was lying out on a chaise thing and I had to hand it to her. She merely smiled, and said, 'Can we help you?'

"Greg came to and introduced us, and I apologized for the intrusion. I said a mutual friend had told me that Greg was in Chatham and suggested I look him up."

"Did she believe you?"

"I doubt it," Florence said honestly, "but she was too well bred to even raise an eyebrow. She insisted that I have a drink, and Greg nearly dropped the glass trying to make me one. We chatted about the Cape and the weather and finally I said I had a date in Provincetown, and Greg took the cue and did the polite thing and walked me to my car. I gave him the name of the place in Hyannis where I was staying and told him it would be in his best interest if he came over that evening."

"Did he?"

"Yes. Greg was always one to do anything that would be in his best interest. I told him about Lisa, and I will say that he was thoroughly shaken. Finally he agreed to meet me in New York in early September and we went to a lawyer who arranged for us each to pay a certain amount per month for Lisa. Greg also took out an insurance policy so that she would be protected in the event of his death."

"And Lisa is still the beneficiary?"

"Yes. But if Greg committed suicide, the insurance company won't pay off."

She reached for another of the stale cigarettes and lighted it herself. Her hands had steadied, but the haunted look in her eyes seemed to have deepened.

He reached a decision. He said, "Look, I can see no reason to keep you in suspense about this. From what has been determined I'd say it's not *impossible* that Greg Banning committed suicide, but it's most unlikely. In my opinion, someone killed him."

She drew in her breath sharply, then laughed shakily. She said, "That's the best news I've had in a long time," and added quickly, "I know how terrible that must sound. . . ."

"No," he said, "I can understand how you feel. Once I thought I wanted to be a pediatrician, but kids got to me too deeply. I can deal with them as a part of general practice, but not all of the time. So...."

He poured brandy for both of them. He said, "Now, there's something I'd like to ask you."

"Fair enough."

"When you saw Greg Banning in the studio just before he died, did he really ask you to share the Van Houden commission with him?"

"No."

"Then, you must have had a reason for inventing the story you did."

"Protection," she said simply. "If I had told the truth, it would have exposed Lisa. I've spent a good part of the past twenty-plus years keeping my secret, doctor. I wasn't about to tell the world now.

"Though," she added this very thoughtfully, "somehow it doesn't seem to matter as much as it did about whether people know about Lisa or not. It seems as if we go to such lengths to conceal things only to realize later that it might have been better to have had it out in the open from the very beginning."

"Blackmailers wouldn't make much money that way," he observed.

She said, quickly defensive, "I wasn't trying to blackmail Greg."

"I wasn't thinking of you."

"Well," she said, sniffing the brandy, "I suppose when you come down to it, in a sense I suppose I have been blackmailing him all these years. That's what it amounts to, really. I threatened to expose the whole sorry story if he didn't pay his share toward our daughter."

"Would it have mattered that much to him if you had?"

"Yes, strangely enough. Greg had tremendous vanity. He painted himself, mentally this is, in larger-than-life Nordic strokes. The concept of his spurning his own idiot child—" and she spoke the words with a cold preciseness "—would not have fit in with the image. Professionally, of course, it wouldn't have made a damned bit of difference.

"Then more recently, there has been Carla. That was a vanity stroke, too. Marriage to a beautiful, much younger woman. Carla was essential to Greg, for as long as he wanted her, though I'm not sure just how much longer that would have been. It doesn't really matter, as things turned out. She is his lawful widow, amen. Whatever he left, she inherits—except for that single insurance policy. That, unless he killed himself, belongs to Lisa, which brings us back to my original point. So, since I respect your opinion, I only hope you are right."

She stood. She said, "I've taken up more than enough of your time, and you've been very generous."

He set his brandy snifter down and said carefully, "Florence, while you were with Greg Banning in the studio did he drink anything?"

"Yes," she said. "I've already told Chief Higgins. He had an odd old bottle in a cabinet, and he took it out and refilled the glass he had brought in with him."

"How was his mood?"

"Exuberant. He didn't even seem to mind that he had lost the Van Houden commission to me."

"Was the meeting in the studio your idea or his?"

"His, but I welcomed it," she said frankly. "He hadn't given me a cent for Lisa since early summer, so when I saw him head for the studio I followed him. He was just filling his glass when I came in.

"I told him I wanted to talk about Lisa and he said frankly he was too high, but he'd meet me any time I wanted the next day, Labor Day. He looked at me and he said, 'Christ, you know you're still beautiful!' Then he added, 'Rich, too, or you will be when you get through with the Van Houdens.'

"I started to tell him that I hadn't set out deliberately to undercut him with the Van Houdens, but before I could, Greg got this terrible expression on his face and he said, 'Flor, I'm *sick*!'

"He lurched for the bathroom—that's the only word I can think of to describe the way he moved—and I could hear him retching. I stood there paralyzed, the change had been so sudden. Then, after a few minutes, he came back. He smiled at me in a funny way and he said, 'Fuzzy. . . Christ, I can hardly *see* you. . . but better.'

"He, well, he groped for his glass, which was empty by then, and then he found that old bottle and he filled the glass very carefully. Then he smiled at me and said, 'Bottoms up' and drank. I suppose I was just staring at him, then all of a sudden it seemed as if his eyes rolled back in his head and he slumped down right at my feet.

"I knew I had to get help, and quickly. I ran outside, looking for you, really, but I didn't see you, so I went to Carla. There were a lot of people around and I didn't want everyone converging on the studio all at once. I tried to tell her quietly that Greg seemed ill and needed her, and she went right in. . . ."

Florence said slowly, "If this *is* murder, I don't envy the police. They'll have quite a job finding out who did it. There must be so many people who've wanted, at one time or another, to kill Greg Banning!"

16

DR. CASEY STOPPED at Olson's Package Store to replenish his liquor supply toward noon on Friday and found Mary Blodgett sitting behind the counter knitting. She scuttled to her feet when she saw him, thrusting yarn and needles into her old capacious tapestry tote bag.

He smiled. "What are you making, Mary?"

"An afghan for the church bazaar. I've got to have it done by Halloween and I'm still on the first strip with six strips still to go."

He laughed. "Do you ever rest?"

"Resting breeds mischief," Mary said.

"Well, then. You're keeping the store?"

"Frank's out back inventorying," she said. "He thinks someone's been getting into the stock."

"Oh?"

"Nothing big, a bottle here, a bottle there. It's the summer help, if you ask me, some of the kids he took on to make deliveries. They could help themselves to a bottle now and again without anyone being the wiser."

"You haven't taken up with the stuff, have you?" he teased, knowing her teetotaling tendencies.

"It'll never touch my lips," she assured him. "Breeds nothing but misery, if you ask me."

"Then I'll have to choose being miserable," he told her. "I'll take a bottle of Jack Daniels, please, and I guess I'd better have some Scotch, too."

"You planning to entertain?" she asked him.

"No. But people do stop by occasionally."

"Half the women in town would, if they did what they'd like to do," Mary told him, and insisted she was right, despite his protests.

She made change, and was back at her knitting by the time he left.

He had parked near the back of the store and he noticed that the door to the rear storage room was open. As he neared it, Frank Olson came out, carrying several empty cardboard cartons.

"Mary do all right by you?" he asked.

Dr. Casey nodded. "She always does."

Olson grinned. "For someone who hates the stuff, she's right with it," he said. "She can even tell you the right wine for the right occasion."

"She said you're inventorying," Casey said.

"End-of-the-season damage survey," Olson said. "You have to expect to be ripped off to a certain amount by the summer help, but I still like to tally it up."

The liquor-store owner was a dark, stocky man who affected a barbershop-quartet mustache. He was pleasant enough when he was sober, but Dr. Casey knew that on those rare occasions when Olson dipped into his own stock the results could

be catastrophic. He was noted for both his hot
temper and his slugging ability.

He said now, "I still got a half a case of that
stuff Banning drank. *Cassis*. That'll be sitting on
the shelf for a long day, or I miss my guess.
Funny thing, though. Maybe the kids go for it,
because there's a bottle missing."

"Really?"

"Yeah. The past few years I've ordered a case
of it toward spring, to be sure it would be here by
the time Banning came up. He's always bought it
a bottle at a time, and even with the amount of
drinking he did, a bottle of something like *cassis*
goes a hell of a long way."

"How much *had* he used?"

"Well, I figured it out for Chief Higgins," Olson
said. "That is, I *thought* I'd figured it out for
Chief Higgins. I usually keep two bottles out on
the shelves, just in case anyone might be interested. They're still there. Matter of fact,
they're left over from last year, which means
that I added twelve bottles to my stock, and I still
got four. I thought that meant Banning had used
up eight."

"How do you know he didn't?"

"He charged everything he bought and he had
it delivered," Olson said. "I've checked my
records and he's only had seven bottles of *cassis*
sent out since he came up here. Hadn't paid for
them, either."

"Couldn't someone else have bought the
eighth bottle?" Dr. Casey asked.

Olson shook his head. "If anyone had just come

in off the street to buy a bottle of *cassis*, it would have come off the shelf, and the same two bottles are still there. That means the missing bottle came out of the stockroom.''

''Were any of your summer help French?''

''No. Why?''

''Well, *cassis* is rather popular in France.''

''It isn't popular here,'' Olson said. ''I can't remember when anyone except Banning has asked for it.''

''Have you told the chief about this?''

''Yes. I called him.''

Casey frowned. He said, ''Wouldn't Bart Smith have taken a bottle of *cassis* out to Banning's party with him?''

''No,'' said Olson. ''I furnished the liquor for the rest of the crowd but Banning always put out his own brew. He had this funny bottle he kept it in—''

''I know,'' said Casey.

''I even checked with Banning before the party,'' Olson said. ''Because I wanted to give him a gentle hint about his overdue bill. He said he had plenty of his 'mixture,' as he called it.''

''When did you last deliver *cassis* to him?''

''The first of August,'' Olson said promptly. ''I looked that up, too.''

''I don't suppose you remember how many bottles were left in the case after that first of August delivery?''

''No, I just knew I wasn't running low.'' Olson shrugged. ''Like I told the chief, I got beer and wine missing and maybe these same kids who took it figured the *cassis* was some sort of wine and helped themselves."

After leaving the liquor store, Dr. Casey stopped briefly at Jessie's Kitchen for a cheeseburger, then remembered that the tide would be high toward late afternoon, and wondered if Paul Chase might be interested in a little flounder fishing.

He drove down Fuller Road, thinking that there might be just enough time to walk across to the Chases and ask Paul before office hours started, but as he swung into his own driveway, this hope vanished.

Carla Banning's white Porsche was parked directly in front of his office door.

He pulled up behind it and got out, dreading an encounter with her. He had not seen Carla since the memorial service on Wednesday and he wondered now just how he was going to handle her.

It surprised him that she had come here; it was more her style to issue a summons.

He moved toward her car reluctantly and it was not until he had almost reached it that he looked up and stopped short, unable to camouflage his surprise.

Clare, not Carla, sat in the driver's seat. She was wearing a floppy white sun hat that hid her copper hair and he was aware for the first time of certain physical similarities between the two sisters; their profile, the way they tilted their heads with a certain imperiousness. Even though Clare was smaller and very different in coloring, he had, at a distance, been fooled.

She was wearing oversized sunglasses. Now she took them off and her blue eyes were dazzling. She laughed shortly, and she said, "You do wear your heart on your sleeve, don't you!"

He was honestly puzzled. "What do you mean?"

"Well, you're not exactly a welcoming committee, Dr. Casey. I watched you, walking over here. You have a rather transparent face. I should think physicians would have to be rather careful about things like that."

She was being nasty again, or very nearly nasty. He looked down at her, not giving a damn at the moment if his face *was* transparent. His throat constricted, and he was swept by a feeling that was part anger, part frustration. It seemed to him that he had been at a disadvantage with her ever since they met because of either Gregory or Carla Banning, and he resented it. He closed his eyes briefly and opened them again to find her watching him closely, with a rather revealing expression of her own that he cataloged somewhere between concern and anxiety.

She said, "You look awfully tired."

"I am," he admitted.

He glanced at his watch. "Look," he said, "would you like to come in before I start acquiring patients?"

"No," she said, and added quickly, "I had to go uptown for a few things and Carla asked me to stop by. She wondered if you'd come for dinner tonight. She's asked Tony Mayo and the Baileys. I think she's trying to fill in a few hours. It's like living under a cloud, and I suppose it will be until it's definite about Greg's death.''

"What about you?''

"About me?''

"Are you going to stay here with her?''

He had noticed before that she had a way of raising her eyebrows when surprised. She said, "You sound as if you think I shouldn't.''

"I'm not sure that you should,'' he countered.

She looked at him curiously. She said, "If you weren't about to have office hours and I didn't have errands to do, I'd pursue that. As it is, may we expect you around six?''

17

IT WAS A GOLDEN EVENING. Barring a hurricane, the Cape would be coming into its best time over these next few weeks. With October, the stripers would be striking again along the Outer Beach, and there would still be trout fishing in the ponds, flounder fishing and clamming. The water, in the bay and the ponds at least, would still be warm enough for swimming, and there would be lazy weekend afternoons to sail or to go for hikes along the trails in the National Seashore.

Driving across town to Heights Road and the Banning house, Dr. Casey found himself wishing that he had someone to share all of this with, and it was not at all difficult to promote a vision of a small person with chicory-blue eyes and copper hair.

Too bad, he thought with a rueful smile as he turned in the Banning driveway, that it was not Clare who had succumbed to a doctor fixation, rather than her sister!

He was the last to arrive. Tony and the Baileys already had been supplied with drinks, and Carla promptly said, "Jack Daniels for you, darling?"

He winced at the "darling," even though it was just a pattern of speech with Carla. He glanced across at Clare and it seemed to him that she smiled faintly. A moment later she passed a tray of appetizers to him and he took one and ate it absently before he realized it was an anchovy, and he detested anchovies.

Carla gave him his drink, managing to make the touch of her fingers as she handed him the glass akin to a caress. Her color was better tonight, and she seemed reasonably sober.

The drapes had been drawn back from the glass windows that fronted the long, narrow living room, and the view defied description. Although he had seen it many times before, Casey found himself committed to it again; it became hypnotic when you loved the sea as he did.

Clare said, at his elbow, "All the way to Portugal. At least, it seems as if you can see that far, doesn't it?"

To his surprise, she perched on a hassock at the side of his chair. She was wearing a yellow pantsuit, her hair tied back with a band of the same color, and she looked fresh and young and very lovely.

She said, "I owe you an apology, doctor. I never even waited today to find out whether or not you could come."

"I noticed," he admitted, and she smiled.

She said, "Then thanks for being generous enough to come anyway."

Their eyes met; she was the first to look away, biting her lip as she did so. Things were not as they seemed on the surface with Clare, he realized now.

Tony, Carla and the Baileys were engaged in an animated discussion on the other side of the room. Under cover of it he said, lowering his voice, "I wish you'd tell me."

"Tell you what?"

"Whatever it is."

She looked out to sea, her eyes seeming to trace the eternal blue to the horizon and beyond. Then she said, her own voice lowered, "Would you believe. . .I want to? Could you take me to breakfast tomorrow morning?"

He tried not to stare at her. He said, guardedly, "If it's early enough. I do have a couple of house calls to make midmorning."

"As early as you like," she said. "How about seven? I get up at dawn, anyway. It's Carla who's the late sleeper. I'll meet you in the drugstore parking lot."

Carla, attuned to the sound of her own name, called out, "What's that about Carla?"

"I was telling Dr. Casey our supper tonight's a communal effort," Clare fibbed. "You made the salad and I made the quiche."

Plates and silverware had been laid out on the dining-room table; candles flickered in long silver holders. The supper was served buffet and Casey, helping himself, glanced at the corner cabinet. The spot where the Moses bottle had stood was vacant, which meant that the bottle and its companion, too, undoubtedly, were still residing at police headquarters.

The party broke up at ten o'clock when Tony Mayo got a phone call. When he came back into the living room after answering it Dr. Casey looked his question, and Tony said promptly, "Not for you. An elderly lady—heart—her own physician was in attendance. But," he said reluctantly, "I'll have to go."

They had been thrusting death out all evening; now it entered despite them. Tony left and Carla poured herself another drink, telling the others to help themselves.

Hank Bailey said, "I know they say undertakers make a fortune, but I'm damned if I'd want his job."

"Someone has to do it," Jane Bailey said practically.

"Someone has to do a lot of things," said her husband. "That doesn't make them any more desirable."

Dr. Casey stood up. "It's been a long day," he said, somewhat apologetically.

"Oh, come *on*," Carla insisted. "One for the road, everybody."

Hank Bailey said, "Okay, but just a short one."

Casey sat down again, and Clare brought him some Jack Daniels and water. As she handed him the glass he noticed that her fingers were cold.

The conversation became stilted. They finished their drinks, and now the Baileys rose to leave, too. They went out through the kitchen, this a Cape Cod custom that was especially practical in this case as it brought them closer to where they had parked their cars. At the last minute Carla called, and reluctantly Casey went back to where she stood in the doorway.

"Lon," she said, "I could use some sleeping pills."

"Not when you're drinking," he said firmly.

"There must be *something*."

"I'd rather you go take a walk on the beach, and see what nature can do for you."

She said plaintively, smiling yet more than half meaning it, "Don't be so cruel."

Behind them, they could hear Hank Bailey trying to start his car. The engine coughed and sputtered, coughed and sputtered, and finally he got out and slammed the door and said, "The battery, damn it."

Casey said quickly, "I'll give you a ride."

Jane Bailey got in the middle of the front seat, and Hank slid in beside her. "Damned car," he said. "I told you to get that battery checked, Jane."

Casey, behind the wheel now, could feel her body tense. She said sharply, "That's right. Blame it on me."

"Well," said Hank, being very reasonable about it, "it *is* your car."

"What about yours?" she asked, elaborately polite.

"Oh, the hell with it," Bailey said sourly.

Jane laughed. "He creamed his car night before last, doctor, after Greg Banning's funeral. Hank got drunk as a coot. It's a good thing there were some other people around to get the paper out or we never would have made it."

"Christ," said Hank, "I worked till midnight. What more do you want?" He laughed shortly. "Everyone thinks it's such a breeze, owning a Cape Cod weekly. Well, you can have it! Want to buy a tired newspaper, doctor?"

They had turned off Heights Road onto Main Street. Dr. Casey said, "I'm afraid I wouldn't know what to do with it."

"Neither does Hank, sometimes," said Jane. "That's when he tries to escape into his ivory tower, and would you believe there's only one escape route? The good old bottle. The Cape must be studded with ivory tower bottles."

Hank said, briefly, "You're tiresome, Jane."

"No more than you are, dear," she said. And Dr. Casey began to wish that he had let the Baileys walk home.

He said, "You'll have to tell me where to turn off for your house."

"We're out toward Snow Harbor, off Aunt Mary's Road," Jane said. "Pussy Willow Lane. Sounds romantic, doesn't it."

Hank, who had lapsed into a morose silence, snorted, but Jane persisted. "When we first came here, it *was* romantic," she said. "Our house is an old Cape, and there were wild roses all over the place. It was June, I remember how utterly captivated I was. Hank and I had been living in a one-room studio in Greenwich Village. This was another world. I thought I'd die of happiness." She paused. "I wish I had," she said.

"Oh, fuck it!" said Hank irritably.

"That shows you were never meant to be a writer," Jane said smugly.

"What the hell do you mean by that?"

"When you have to resort to four-letter words it's a sign of a limited vocabulary."

"You can fuck that, too," said Hank. Then, after a moment, he added, slowly, "I've never had any illusions about myself as a writer. I've written crap for the paper just because somebody had to do it, you know that."

"But all the while what you really wanted was a studio full of paints and easels and models, wasn't it, darling?" Jane asked sweetly. "You wanted to play at being Greg Banning."

The atmosphere changed and now there was steel in it; raw cold. Hank said very quietly, "No, I never wanted to play at being Greg Banning."

"I don't know," Jane said. "You went into mourning Wednesday. At least that's what it seemed like. You didn't stop drinking from the moment we got back from the memorial service. What was it for? Greg, or just your lost youth?"

"Neither," said Hank, "and it wasn't I who was in mourning. You mourn lost loves, or what might have been. You've got things switched, Jane. That was you."

It was less than three miles from The Heights to Aunt Mary's Road, but the distance seemed eternal. Dr. Casey turned off Main Street, turned onto Aunt Mary's Road, and said, "You'll have to tell me just where Pussy Willow Lane comes in."

"Just past the next white house on the right," said Jane. "It's not paved."

He rounded a curve, slowed as he saw the white house, his headlights picked out the road—little more than a dirt track, really—and they bumped down it till Jane said, "There, on the left."

Hank opened the car door and said, "Thanks, doctor," and went on up the narrow path to the house without a backward glance. Jane started to follow him and then turned back. She stood by the car and she made a wistful figure in the moonlight. Silver etched her hair and the planes of her face; she had unusually good features, Dr. Casey thought; as a younger woman she must have been close to beautiful.

She said, "I'm sorry we both bitched so much. It's been a rough week."

He glanced up at her, but night veiled her eyes. He remembered Tony Mayo saying that he had seen Jane go into the studio with Greg at the party. Had it been for old times' sake, or for some entirely different reason?

18

CLARE WAS at the drugstore parking lot when Dr. Casey got there Saturday morning. She left her car and slipped into the seat next to him before he could even make the gesture of getting out and opening the door for her.

She said, "Do you suppose we could get out of Devon?"

"There's a little place out in Wellfleet," he suggested. "I'm sure they'd still be open."

"That would be good."

Dr. Casey found himself wishing that they could have the whole day together. Then he could take her on out to Provincetown, where they could browse around the narrow streets and watch the fishing boats out on the wharf, and when hunger indicated, stop for Portuguese soup, which he considered the best soup in the world.

She said, "It was kind of you to agree to meet me like this."

Kind of him! He couldn't answer her immediately, something seemed to have gone wrong with his word-selection process.

They circled the traffic rotary at Orleans. Blue

water sparkled to the right, and Clare said, "It's all so beautiful."

He said, "I wish there were time to show it to you, before you go back to New York."

Silence stretched between them. She said slowly, "*I* wish we'd met somewhere else, under different circumstances."

"We did," he said gently. "At Carla's, that is, before this all happened. We simply didn't take advantage of it, that's all."

She shook her head. "No. The *situation* was there all the while," she said, "the tension between Greg and Carla. The only good times were when I was painting with Greg, and that was not because of Greg the man, as I've already told you. It was because of Greg the artist, or rather, what was left of that part of him. He was still a great teacher. He could see beauty as few people do. That was one of his problems. He was too receptive to beauty."

"To women, also?"

"To women, too, yes, but not just to women. To everything. When things didn't seem beautiful enough, Greg turned to enhancers; to drugs, alcohol. You may not agree with that medically, but he said drugs, especially certain kinds of drugs, heightened things for him, colors particularly. He said colors became so intense, for instance, you could hardly bear the beauty of it. He wanted me to share it."

"And you?"

"I didn't want to. Maybe I was afraid, I don't know. I *do* know that I think people become too dependent upon too many things, and it scares me.''

She laughed. She said, ''I'll be confessing my innermost thoughts to you in another minute. Do people always talk to you like this? But then, I suppose being a doctor is almost the next thing to being a priest.''

It was the second time in much too short a space that a woman had tried to equate him with the clergy, and he said, protesting, ''Please! I was never meant to be a priest!''

She was looking straight ahead as she said, ''But you've never married again.''

He was astonished. ''No, I never have,'' he managed to say, keeping his voice level with an effort.

He glanced across at her, and she was still staring straight ahead.

''Was it a happy marriage?'' she asked him.

And he answered, without even stopping to think, ''No.''

This was something that he had never fully admitted before, even to himself, and he was shaken. He said hastily, ''She was a wonderful person. It was my fault, actually. I was in medical school and then interning and in residency, and I was so damned busy. Before I had time to make it up to her she was. . . dead.''

''If it had been right, you wouldn't have needed time to make it up,'' Clare said, her voice very small. ''I know. I had time to make it up, and I couldn't. You can't create what isn't there in the first place. So. . . don't blame yourself.''

They had come to Wellfleet, he turned into the
restaurant parking lot, and stared down at her.
She had averted her face so that all he could see
was her lovely copper hair.

He started to speak, but she opened the car
door and got out, and started toward the restaurant, her back very straight. He got out quickly and went after her.

They were given a corner table and a waitress
who reminded him of Mary Blodgett brought coffee. Clare, stirring hers, said, "Please—excuse
me, will you? I had no intention of getting so personal."

He said softly, "No, I'm not going to excuse
you." And, as she raised her blue eyes, swiftly,
"I needed someone to say that. You did me a
favor. So thank you, but let's not talk about it
anymore, for now. Agreed?"

"Agreed."

He added sugar to his coffee. He said gently, "I
think you should tell me why you asked me to
meet you this morning."

She smiled faintly. "Back to reality? Well, I
suppose we have to. I suppose you might say,
too, that the main reason I asked you to meet me
was that I've misjudged you, and I thought it
only fair to admit it to you."

"Misjudged me?"

"Yes. When you came to the house the other
morning—in the middle of the night, really—I did
think that you and Carla had a rendezvous. You
see, I know that there's been another man all

along. You asked me what was bothering me—
and that's it.''

Clare's eyes met his levelly. She said, "I know
Carla finds you tremendously attractive; she told
me so, she even said she's in love with you. But
she's also told me that you are still in love with
your wife, and she thinks there would always be
a shadow between you and anyone else.''

His eyebrows shot upward. "Oh?"

"That is what discouraged her," Clare said
without looking at him. "Even though I know
there are moments when it seems as if she's still
trying. But Carla wants someone who will be
totally hers. Greg never was. It's mostly when
she has been drinking that she still tries you
again, only it never works. Right?''

"Right," he admitted uncomfortably.

"Well," Clare said, "at some point Carla
turned elsewhere. I don't know just when, or
with whom, but it's almost certainly someone in
Devon. I've gone over the cast of potential
characters and there really aren't very many.
Tony Mayo is attractive—''

"No," Casey interrupted, "I can't quite see
that. I don't mean to say Tony isn't attractive,
but he and Carla. . . .''

"Well, personally, I'd never be sure about anyone," Clare said.

"I suppose you're right," he conceded.

"There's Brent Nickerson," she went on.
"He's fantastically handsome, and he's the type
who would fawn all over a woman.''

Dr. Casey grinned. "He could even sing her love songs in a glorious tenor voice?"

Clare laughed. "I've heard about his voice but I've never heard it. I know, though, that he has spoken to Carla about acting with that drama group next year."

"The Scallopers?" Casey asked.

"Yes. Are they really any good?"

"Surprisingly so, for amateurs."

The waitress brought their breakfasts and Casey absently poured maple syrup on his pancakes. "Who else is there?" he asked.

"Hank Bailey, possibly," Clare said. "He called Carla the other day just to see if there was anything he could do, at least that's what he said. I answered the phone and I recognized his voice. It has a rather odd, scratchy quality."

Clare attended to her own French toast. Then she said, "There's one more: Greg's attorney, Robert Fawcett. He has been around quite a bit. It could be because of Greg's business affairs, but it could also be more than that."

"All right," Dr. Casey said, "suppose Carla *is* involved with one of the people you've mentioned? Is it really important?"

"I think so," Clare admitted. "She's been pretty cautious the past couple of days. She's still drinking, but not so much. I don't think she wants to get out of control again the way she was when she called you the other morning. Also, I keep having the feeling that she's waiting for something."

"What do you think it is?"

"I don't know, but I think every time I go out of the house she calls someone on the phone. The other day I forgot a letter I was going to mail and came back for it. She was dialing and when she saw me she hung up and made some sort of excuse. Each time I go for a walk recently I have the feeling she's up there watching me, while she talks on the phone, so she can be sure to hang up before I come back in the house. This isn't all imagination," Clare said. "A couple of times I've caught a flash of color at the window—and yes, the color does turn out to match whatever dress Carla's wearing."

Clare put down her fork, she said, "Carla's life is her own; we've always been as different as two people possibly could be. I can't understand why she would be so secretive. Even if she wants to run off with someone, that's her business."

"Suppose she did run off with someone," Casey suggested. "How would it affect her financially?"

"I don't know," Clare admitted. "I think pitting Greg's debts against his assets is going to be quite a game."

"Then don't you think Carla's prime interest may be in a man with money, rather than a man for his own sake?"

"I don't know," Clare said. "She's a romantic, believe it or not. If the man happened to be rich, that would be frosting on the cake, of course. Anyway, none of the men we've mentioned is poor, are they?"

"I doubt it," Casey admitted. "I don't know about Robert Fawcett. . . ."

"I imagine he's still realizing a profit on his first dime!"

"Well, then. Tony *is* fairly well heeled. Not because of his business—all undertakers aren't that rich, but he did inherit quite a bit. I don't know that much about Brent Nickerson's financial status. Bankers on the Cape tend to reap prestige in exchange for a poor salary, but it may or may not matter with Nickerson. He may have an independent income. Any permanent alliance with Hank Bailey would first involve divorce from Jane, so I don't know about that. Jane has worked too hard at their business not to get her full share."

"Maybe there would be enough for both of them," Clare suggested.

"Maybe."

Clare's face was very solemn. She said, "If one of them actually had killed for her and then Carla *did* manage to liquidate the house and come out with some cash there might be a certain obligation on her part, wouldn't you say? Even, perhaps, a prearranged agreement?"

He stared at her. "What are you saying?"

"Carla was miserably unhappy with Greg, and he wouldn't give her a divorce. She asked for one months ago, and he laughed in her face.

"You see, Greg was a scalp collector. It would have been unthinkable to him to let a beautiful woman walk out on him. Carla was a beautiful possession. He owned her, he intended to keep it

that way, and he could have made it very rough
for her, unbearably rough, if she had tried to ini-
tiate a divorce without his agreement. Greg was
quite a torture expert.

"So you see," Clare said, "that's what terrified
me so at first, the other night. I thought she'd
killed him. But now I think some other poor, mis-
guided soul did it for her!"

19

Dr. Casey was late in making his house calls that Saturday morning and he got back to his office just as the first patient was parking in front of the door. There was no time throughout the balance of the day to review his conversation with Clare.

He had dropped her off at the drugstore parking lot before going back to his office, and it seemed to him, when she thanked him, that some of the tension had gone out of her face. Her blue eyes were clear and direct, and she seemed the epitome of candor, which only intensified his own feeling of disappointment. For with all her talk about Carla, she had not confided in him about the Moses bottle or her part in hiding it.

When she had crept down to the beach the morning after the murder, and hid it along the edge of the dunes, there had been no talk of a suspicion of methyl-alcohol poisoning, no reason to think that the glass figure of the bearded prophet had in any way been involved in Gregory Banning's death.

Why then, had Clare gone to such lengths to hide the bottle unless she knew something?

Also, ironically, this particular Moses bottle had been proven innocent, anyway. No trace of poison had been found in it, which made Clare's action all the more mysterious.

The last patient gone, Dr. Casey began to think of this as he methodically emptied ashtrays, plumped pillows, straightened magazines, then went back through the breezeway into the kitchen.

Bert Higgins was sitting at the round, maple table reading the newspaper.

"Well," said Casey, "what is this? Entry without a search warrant?"

"People should lock their doors," the chief said succinctly. "Not that it matters that much. If someone really wants to get in, they'll get in."

"That's for publication?"

"The hell it is!" said the chief.

Casey got out the Jack Daniels, the glasses and the ice.

Bert Higgins looked at the liquor, said, "It's getting to be a habit."

"There are times when it's therapeutic," Casey said. He did the necessary things, handed a glass to the chief. "What brings you here?" he asked.

"The need to escape," Higgins admitted. "Brigham's breathing down my neck. He wants a case. He wants to get up in the courtroom and give evidence. He's a frustrated D.A."

Dr. Casey shrugged. "So he'll have to wait. We don't even have the autopsy report back yet."

"That's a poor excuse," the chief said. "We

know Banning was poisoned. We even know
what kind of poison. We even know how.''

"To a point."

"Yes, to a point."

Casey pulled up a chair. "It comes to a matter
of motive," he said, sitting down.

"What do you mean by that?"

"Find out why it was necessary to kill Banning,
and you'll be on the track of who."

Higgins snorted. "Christ," he said, "if you're
looking for motives I can give you a whole plat-
terful of them. From the way I figure it, just
about everyone who ever knew Banning would
just as soon have seen him dead. He left a lot of
hate around."

"I think it was more than that," Dr. Casey said.

"Usually hate is enough," the chief pointed
out. "Motives don't have to be complicated,
Pete. Murder grows out of something bare and
raw. You don't have to get fancy."

"Well, then," Casey asked, "who do we
have?" And the moment he posed the question
he wished he hadn't spoken.

"We have the whole kit and kaboodle," said
the chief. "Our killer *could* be someone
who drove to New York or Boston that same
night or took a plane to San Francisco or wherever, but I don't think so. I think it's one of the
cozy little group we've been talking about all this
time."

Higgins shifted his position and looked uncomfortable, as he always did when he had to say
something he didn't want to say. "Pete," he

blurted finally, "you know these people. I have the feeling you know a little more about them than you've been telling me. That doesn't help."

Higgins was a friend, a good one, and Clare Evans, whether he liked it or not, was a question mark to some extent. But still Dr. Casey proceeded cautiously. "Okay," he said, "Let's take them one by one."

"Who do you want to start with?"

"How about Carla?"

The chief sampled his drink. He said, "I've talked to her three times or more since this happened and I still can't make her out. If you can, tell me."

"She's pushing thirty," said Casey. "That's young enough for most people, but not for a model. Not, at least, the kind of model Carla was when Banning married her. She was doing very well then, both professionally and financially, but for all her glamour she was still essentially a small-town girl from upstate New York. Her sister was studying at the art school where Banning was teaching at the time. One afternoon Carla stopped by to pick up Clare, and Clare introduced her to Banning. Banning recognized her. You couldn't ride a subway, turn on a TV or open a mazagine in those days without seeing Carla's face.

"She was even more beautiful than she is now. Banning saw her as another feather for his cap. He wanted her. He got her.

"That was six or seven years ago. Banning—and remember, Bert, this may not be strictly

accurate, I'm putting together pieces when I tell
you this—Banning had already bought the place
on The Heights. He and Carla came here summers,
and it was great, at first. Then there were other
women, drugs—in which he involved Carla when
she didn't want to be involved—a lot of partying,
a lot of drinking. Banning was beginning to lose
his grip as an artist. He insulted his clients and
fewer of them were inclined to take his guff, especially when his work was no longer up to its
former quality. He started to lose commissions,
money.

"Finally, Carla wanted out, but he wouldn't let
her go. He refused a divorce, and I'm sure he made
it clear she wouldn't get a cent if she left him.
Doubtless he pointed out that time had passed,
she wasn't as young as she used to be, she'd
drenched herself with liquor and she wouldn't
have a prayer of functioning as a model in today's
market, all of which is true. So she settled for the
status quo."

"Or," the chief said, "for a pint or so of
poison?"

"I hope not," Dr. Casey admitted. "Speaking of
pints of poisons—for no good reason, the phrase
brings to my mind the fact that Tony Mayo says he
saw Jane Bailey go into the studio with Greg not
too long before he died."

"I know," the chief said. "He told me, and I
tried to get around to it the other afternoon when
I stopped by at the paper. Both she and Hank were
there working and she steered clear of the sub-

ject, I could tell she wasn't about to admit anything with Hank around.

"I got her at home alone, the next morning. She told me Banning asked her to look at a picture he wanted her to see, and so she went into the studio with him. She insists that's all there was to it, but she doesn't want Bailey to know about it even now. I gather Banning has been a very sore point with Bailey."

"Yes," Casey said, "and evidently for many reasons. If it's true that Banning had an affair with Jane you have a case of an aggrieved husband. Also, Bailey had been insulted by Banning professionally on more than one occasion. Did Jane say what sort of a picture he wanted to show her?"

"She said it was a picture of a girl. She didn't elaborate. She gave the impression that Banning had asked her before to look at his work. Who knows? Maybe he valued her opinion."

"Jane is smart," Casey admitted, "but I don't see her as an art critic. Especially for Banning."

"Neither did I," the chief conceded. "It wasn't the moment to push, though. Funny thing about Bailey, incidentally. He was the one who got Banning to come to Devon in the first place."

"Really?"

"Yeah. Bailey had moved up here from New York, married Jane, and they started the paper together. The house on The Heights came up for sale, the man who owned it had got in over his head, needed instant money. Bailey knew this, and right about then he happened to pick up a magazine Banning had done the cover for. Bailey says an idea clicked. He remembered that Banning had been on the Cape one summer and had been very taken by it, so he put through a call to him. Banning came up the next weekend and bought the place."

"Does that mean that Banning and Bailey were friends at the time?"

"I'd guess they were neither friends nor enemies," the chief said. "Maybe there was a commission in the sale for Bailey, who knows? This would be a good ten years ago, before he had even met Carla, and there would have been no affair with Jane then. Maybe Banning wasn't as insulting as he came to be later."

Dr. Casey looked for his pipe, found it and filled it while the chief fixed disapproving eyes upon him. He said slowly, "There's something else, Bert. Something told me in confidence, although I warned the lady I wasn't a priest, and she isn't one of my patients."

"Florence Page?" asked the chief, and Casey nodded.

Then he carefully detailed the basics of his visit from Florence, but not before stressing the point that this was between the two of them, information to be kept away from Lieutenant Brigham unless it had to be otherwise.

The chief sighed when he had finished. "There's another one who could have done without Banning," he said wearily. "Do you suppose he had any friends? His own lawyer, Fawcett, doesn't seem to have had any love for him. Then,

Bart Smith told me that Brent Nickerson and Banning had an argument the evening of the party. Bart couldn't hear what they said, but he says Brent looked furious. Banning just laughed at him. That seems to have been his mood all evening."

"Methyl alcohol tends to work that way in the early stages," Casey said.

Finally the moment came. "What about Mrs. Evans?" the chief asked.

"What about her?" he asked carefully, and was aware that Bert Higgins was eyeing him narrowly, the shrewd blue eyes alert.

"She's got to you, hasn't she, Pete?" he asked gently, and it was this very gentleness that made Dr. Casey more cautious than ever.

"That has no bearing on the case, Bert," he said stiffly.

"I wouldn't say that," the chief disagreed. "It could have a lot of bearing on the case. The lady could be pulling some pretty wool over your eyes. She hid the Moses bottle, remember."

"*A* Moses bottle," Casey corrected. "Not *the* Moses bottle."

"Regardless, she must have had a good reason. People don't do things like that just for the hell of it—not when a murder's just been committed. Don't you agree?"

"I don't know," Casey admitted miserably. The pipe became a losing battle. He put it aside. He said, defensively, "Look, while you're casting suspicions around, how about Tony Mayo? Maybe he had it in for Banning. Or Bertha Murphy?

She worked there, maybe she hated him, too. Or
Mary Blodgett? She also worked there, from time
to time. Even Bart Smith, for that matter? Banning probably owes him a bundle. Or maybe
Frank Olson, over at the liquor store? Banning
owes him, too—''

"Okay, okay," said the chief. "For the moment
we'll lay off Mrs. Evans."

For the moment.

20

IT WAS A LONELY SATURDAY night. Bert Higgins suggested dinner and a movie, saying that he was off duty for the evening, but Dr. Casey had no taste for either. He pleaded the necessity of getting out bills, a task that should have been attended to earlier in the week but he had been staving off. The chief told him he should stop trying to handle everything himself and hire a secretary. He could think of no counter argument at the moment, so Higgins left with a smug smile.

With the chief gone, Casey peered into the freezer compartment of his refrigerator. The stack of TV dinners he kept on hand for such occasions looked decidedly unappetizing, but he selected one at random, put it in the oven, and made himself another drink while it baked.

He watched the rerun of a mystery movie on TV while he ate, read for a while, and then went to bed.

When the telephone rang, he automatically glanced at the luminous dial of his bedside clock, this from long-standing habit. It was 3:00 A.M.

He lifted the receiver reluctantly, answered in

a sleep-edged voice, then came to instant wakefulness when the police dispatcher told him his services as a medical examiner were required at the Watkins cottage on Pine Branch Lane.

He switched on the bed light so that he could see to jot down the directions the dispatcher gave him; the cottage was on the bay side of town, off Main Street, down one road and up another in a true Cape Cod maze. As he hung up and started to dress, he realized that it probably wasn't very far from the Baileys' house.

The streets were deserted at this hour. The stillness emphasized his own tenseness. When you were called out in the middle of the night on an M.E. case it was always a jolt, yet normally he took it in stride. But events, lately, hadn't been normal. Personal feelings and professionalism had been blended, and they didn't mix well.

He had memorized the dispatcher's directions, so now he turned off Main Street, went up one road and down another, then came to a stop when he saw red lights rotating in the darkness. So it was a fire he had been called to, evidently with a related fatality.

A fireman came up to the car, recognized him, and said cheerfully, "Doubt if you can get through, doc. We got the road pretty well blocked. Isn't much of a road anyway."

"No, it isn't," he agreed.

"Had to run a hose over to a pond out back to

get water," the fireman said. "No town water out here."

It was a sparsely settled area, principally small, shingled summer cottages of an older vintage.

Dr. Casey parked his car off the edge of the road, took out his bag and climbed carefully over the fire hoses that seemed to snake everywhere. He saw a police cruiser ahead of him, the blue dome light sweeping, intermittently, across a cottage already starkly highlighted by glaring floodlights.

Bert Higgins detached himself from a group of men and started across to him; he met him halfway. The chief's face was streaked with soot. His eyes, deepset, were gloomy. He said, "It's a nasty one, Pete. Bertha Murphy."

It took a moment for the name of the stout cleaning woman who had worked for Carla, to register.

"Where is she?" he asked.

"Over there," said the chief. "She's dead. I'd say it's smoke inhalation. She doesn't seem to be burned much."

"I'll take a look," he said tersely.

Pine needles scuffled beneath his feet as he walked across the yard. Bertha Murphy was lying at the edge of the pool of light. Someone had covered her with a blanket and Dr. Casey knelt down and turned it back.

She was, indeed, dead, but as the chief had said, she did not seem to have been burned; at least her face had been spared. He covered her again and said to an emergency medical technician standing nearby, "As soon as you can get through, take her to Mayo's."

"We can get through," the technician promised. "This road goes out to Bayberry Road, and we got a police cruiser down at the other end keeping it open."

"Then you might as well get along."

Bert Higgins had come up behind him. "You'll want an autopsy, I suppose?" he said.

"Yes. The cause of death seems obvious, but even so. . . ."

"Hendricks thinks this was arson," said the chief.

At that instant the fire chief appeared and said, "That's right."

Dr. Casey got to his feet again. "Why?" he asked.

"Place reeks of kerosene."

"Is there that much still standing?"

"Quite a bit, matter of fact. Heavy smoke damage. But it's mostly the shed back of the kitchen that burned. Kitchen had quite a bit of damage, too. Rest of the place has some scorching, and we had to break windows, of course."

"Did Bertha Murphy live here alone?"

Chief Higgins nodded. "She had for the past few years, ever since her husband died. For a while she had an apartment on Main Street; they'd up her rent every summer, finally she couldn't keep it. She was too damned proud to go on welfare. She's got a son out in California. I think he sent her a little something every month. She eked out enough to get by on cleaning for people like the Bannings.

"She doesn't own this cottage. Belongs to Bart Smith, matter of fact, he bought it awhile back from some people from Jersey named Watkins. The cottage needed fixing, guess Bart didn't have time to get to it so he let Bertha have the place cheap because she helped him out on some catering jobs now and then. That's what I imagine, anyway. We'll be talking to him, of course."

"Are the other cottages on this road occupied?"

The fire chief answered that one. "They were rented till Labor Day," he said, "but they're empty now."

"So no one else lives near here year-round?"

"I think the nearest year-round houses are out on Bayberry Road," the fire chief said. "Wouldn't you think so, Bert? Depends what you call near, I suppose. There are a lot of shortcut trails around here but you'd need a four-wheel drive to get through most of them without getting stuck."

"Were there any tire prints?" Casey asked.

Chief Higgins smiled ruefully. "If there were, I'm afraid the fire trucks have wiped them out. The county boys will be checking, but I'm not optimistic. Pine needles cover up tracks pretty fast if there's any breeze and this is just one damned pine forest around here."

He turned to the fire chief, "Ted," he said, "you don't need me around here any longer. I'm going to cut out. I'll leave one cruiser at the end of the lane and the other at the Bayberry Road end until you get your equipment out of here."

"Good enough," the fire chief agreed.

Dr. Casey walked back toward his car, and after

pausing briefly to speak to one of his own men Bert Higgins followed him.

The chief said heavily, "This is going to mean another call at the Banning house, and I don't relish it. Bertha Murphy probably cleaned for quite a few people, but I don't know who they were. Maybe Carla Banning can give us a lead."

"I'll ask her for you, if it would help," Casey offered, although he also did not welcome the thought of going back to the Banning house for reasons he could not have clarified to himself, let alone to Bert Higgins.

"It would help," the chief said firmly.

It was four-thirty when Casey got home, thoroughly awake. He thought of a drink, but opted for a cup of hot milk instead, and he took it into his bedroom, settling down in a favorite, worn armchair as he drank it.

There was no point in getting Carla out of bed to answer questions about Bertha Murphy, if indeed she could answer them at all. It would be hours before he could go to see her, but he found himself wishing that in the interim there were some way he could find out more about Bertha Murphy.

Although he would check his records to be sure, he was quite certain that she had never consulted him as a patient, so that was no help.

Tall, angular, primly New England Priscilla Standish, his "part-time housekeeper," was a native of Devon and surely would have known Bertha Murphy. She would be one good source of information, and Mary Blodgett, who was about the same age as the dead woman and had worked with her from time to time, was another. They each might talk more freely to him than they would to Bert Higgins, he told himself, not because of his ego but because it was a fact. Middle-aged—and older—women were touching, often, in their confidence and subsequent confiding in a doctor. The priest bit again, he thought, not without a touch of bitterness.

In any event, once this day was older he would do his bit for Bert Higgins by talking not only to Carla Banning, but to Pris Standish and Mary Blodgett, as well.

HE AWOKE TO FIND the sun streaming through his window, but the sight evoked little joy this morning. He got up, feeling groggy; sometimes poor sleep was worse than no sleep at all and he'd been having a full share of dreams, forgotten, fortunately, with wakefulness.

He glanced at his watch and was astonished to find that it was eight-thirty. The middle of the day!

He quickly dialed Priscilla Standish's number and she answered on the third ring, sounding breathless.

"Did I interrupt something?" he asked her.

"Just getting on my hat," Pris told him. "I'm about to leave for church."

"Nine o'clock service?" Dr. Casey asked.

"Yes."

"Pris, could you stop by here at the house afterward?"

Instantly she was worried. "You sick or something, doctor?" she demanded.

"No, I'm fine." He sighed. He said, "You'll probably hear it at church, anyway. There was a bad fire in Bertha Murphy's house last night. A very bad fire."

He could hear Priscilla suck in her breath at the other end of the line. She said, "That's dreadful. Bertha of all people. Nothing but bad luck."

"She's dead, Pris," he said, wishing he could be more gentle about it.

"Oh, dear God!" Priscilla Standish moaned.

"It happened fast," he said quickly. "Smoke inhalation. She didn't suffer long and she wasn't burned." Then, "Did you know her well, Pris?"

"All my life," said Priscilla. "We went to school together. Bertha and me, Mary Blodgett, too. Didn't see too much of each other later on, the three of us kind of went our own ways. I know Mary better, if you get right down to it. Bertha went to the Catholic Church. Not that I've got anything against Catholics, mind you. She was a good woman." Priscilla sniffled. "Poor Bertha," she said, her voice muffled.

"Look, Pris," he told her, "if no one mentions this to you would you keep it to yourself? I'd appreciate that. I can tell you more when I see you, if you can stop by."

"I'll be there," Priscilla said.

21

PRISCILLA WAS WEARING a royal blue dress with an incredible hat of a matching shade and, incongruously, the same stout, laced, black shoes she wore when she came to work for him.

She sat at the kitchen table, morosely stirring sugar into the cup of coffee he had poured for her, and said, "No one at church said a thing. So I didn't breathe a word."

He could imagine how tempted she had been and he said, "Thanks, Pris. Look, I'm going to have to ask you to keep my confidence again, for the time being. The fire chief thinks this may be arson."

Priscilla stared at him, horrified. She said, "That would be just like murder, doctor. Bertha could hardly get around, with that bad ankle."

He frowned, trying to remember. He said, "I didn't realize she was lame."

"She wasn't. She sprained her ankle just a couple of days ago. She was working at the Baileys and she slipped on their back steps and took a nasty fall. Mrs. Bailey wanted to call you, but Bertha wouldn't hear of it.

"She called us up that night—I think it was

Thursday—and I went over. Her poor foot was swollen up like a balloon. She'd asked me to bring her some epsom salts and she soaked it, then she let me bind it up for her. I wanted to call you myself, but I knew how mad Bertha would be. She had a mind of her own.''

Priscilla put down her coffee spoon with characteristic neatness and said, ''You wouldn't believe it, Bertha'd got so fat and all, but she was voted the prettiest one in our class in school. She had a real good figure in those days. Then she married Mike Murphy and had three kids. . . .''

''Three?''

Priscilla nodded. ''Mike, junior—he's the one lives out in California—and the twins. The twins drowned in Cranberry Pond one winter. They were skating, and they broke right through the ice. You can't never be sure of these ponds on the Cape.''

She was right about that, Dr. Casey conceded. Most of the Cape's many fresh-water ponds were deep holes, kettles left behind long ago by receding glaciers, and they could be dangerous.

''After the twins drowned, Mike Murphy started drinking like a fish,'' Priscilla said, ''and Bertha started putting on the weight. She kind of dropped out of everything and I lost track of her for a while, then I read in the paper one night, a few years back that Mike Murphy had died—heart attack. Naturally I went to the wake, though I guess I was about the only Protestant there. I even went to the mass the next day.

''After that I used to stop in once in a while to

see how she was making out. She and Murphy
had a little place down toward Scallop Cove but
she had to sell it. She moved into an apartment
on Main Street, but each summer the owner
upped her rent, so a year or so ago Bart Smith
said she could move into his cottage. All it had
for heat was a couple of electric space heaters,
but Bertha said she could make out, and she did.

"Bart said the place needed a lot of fixing if he
was going to rent it for a decent price, and he had
so much catering business he couldn't get to it,
but if you ask me I think he just *said* that. Bart
Smith's got a soft heart, though you might not
think it. He helped Bertha get those cleaning
jobs, too, like the one with the Bannings."

"Did you say she worked for the Baileys?"

"Yep. One day a week."

"Who else?"

"Summer people," Priscilla said, "and people
like Florence Page who are here sort of off and
on."

"Bertha worked for Florence Page?"

"Yes. She cleaned for Bart, too, come to think
of it—he's a bachelor. He has a nice place that
looks right out over Snow Harbor."

"Anyone else?"

Priscilla thought for a moment, then said,
"Brent Nickerson, since his wife walked out on
him. She said his place was a *real* mess when she
first went there. He'd been eating out of cans;
he'd just open them and scoop out the food and
there were empty cans all over the kitchen."

Bertha Murphy had worked for the Bannings,

Florence Page, the Baileys, Brent Nickerson, even Barton Smith. These were the very people he and Bert Higgins had been discussing, and the conclusion was inevitable.

Disturbing though it might be, there was a very good possibility that Greg Banning's and Bertha Murphy's deaths were connected.

He frowned. "Didn't Bertha also clean for Tony Mayo?" he asked Priscilla.

"No," she said. "Minnie Doane works for him. She's getting on in years, I don't know how she keeps up, but she says Tony is as neat as a pin and he eats anything she puts before him. She goes over to the funeral parlor sometimes and helps fix people up. She's a whiz at makeup." Priscilla shuddered. "I wouldn't like working on dead people," she said.

Neither does Tony Mayo, Dr. Casey thought, but he didn't voice the thought.

He dialed the Banning house as soon as Priscilla left, and Clare answered the phone.

"Lon," she said, seemingly pleased, "I was hoping you'd call."

"When I tell you my reason you may not say that," he admitted reluctantly.

"Oh?"

"Is Carla around?"

"No, she went over to Chatham for brunch with some friends, but I don't think she'll be away too long. Do you want her to call you?"

"Yes," he said, then amended it. "No. I'll come out around two, if that's all right?"

"It's perfectly all right," Clare said, then he

sensed her hesitation, but it was only momentary.

"Lon," she asked him, "something has happened, hasn't it? What is it?"

He clutched the telephone receiver and briefly closed his eyes, because suddenly he knew that it was all right with Clare—which didn't make sense, and wasn't in the least scientific—but the relief, nevertheless, was overwhelming.

He said, even though this wasn't what he wanted to say to her at all, "There was a fire in Bertha Murphy's house last night. She died in it."

Clare's "Oh," was a little gasp, and he could feel her genuine pain. "Oh, *Lon*," she said. Then, "How did it happen?"

"We don't know yet," he told her. "She lived alone, out in a summer cottage area, and hers was the only house still occupied. We're trying to trace down the people she worked for, to see if they could tell us a little bit about her."

Clare said doubtfully, "I don't imagine Carla knows too much about her. She usually came twice a week to clean and iron, and when Carla had parties she usually came in to do up the dishes."

"Do you know how long she has been working for Carla?"

"No." Clare hesitated. "We never came up here when my husband was alive," she said then. "Harrison always wanted to go places on vacation where he might run into clients; accidentally on purpose, I suppose you'd say. He wasn't interested in Greg's crowd, anyway. For a few years, there, Carla and I saw very little of each other. When I came up here, I rather expected that she'd have full-time help, but I don't think she ever has.''

"How is she doing, actually?'' he asked. ''Is she drinking quite so much? Things seemed better at dinner the other night.''

"I don't know,'' Clare said. ''She isn't drinking so much openly, but she's not a child. I can't watch her all the time, and I can't hide the bottle. . . .''

It was an unfortunate phrase. It hung between them.

"Look,'' Clare said finally, ''come along whenever you want, unless you're busy until two. Come at noon, if you like, and I'll make you a sandwich.''

"I'll take you up on that,'' he told her.

SHE HAD BLOODY MARYS ready when he got there, and although he wasn't usually partial to them they were just right for the moment.

They sat out on the terrace in front of the house where, just a week ago, Barton Smith's impromptu bar had been set up. She asked him about the fire at Bertha Murphy's house and noted that once again he had been up since before dawn. He smiled slightly and said there wasn't anything too unusual about that, and she said, ''But you seem to be on call so much of the time. There should be others to share the burden.''

Until now, he had *sought* the burden to fill the hours, and he nearly told her so. Then, without even looking at her, he knew he didn't have to tell her so. She already knew.

They had a second Bloody Mary, then she brought out sandwiches and iced coffee. As she set the tray on a table in front of him she disconcerted him completely by saying, "You know about the bottle, don't you?"

His expression gave him away and she smiled rather sadly. She said, "Chief Higgins asked me to stop by his office yesterday, and I did. He told me they'd found it, in fact, that one of his men saw me hide it in the first place."

Her eyes searched his face. "Didn't the chief tell you he'd talked to me?" she asked him.

"No."

She looked puzzled. She said, "I thought he would, but regardless, I wanted you to know about it, Lon. It was a panic reaction, that's the only way I can describe it. After you gave Carla a shot that morning and she went to sleep I sat there by myself in the living room and it just seemed to hit me, all of a sudden. I remembered the bottle in Greg's studio. He always kept two of them filled with that brew of his, one in the house, one in the studio.

"I thought to myself, it won't be the one on the bar that has the poison in it, it will be the one in the studio. So I, well, I went over to the studio and got the other bottle and ran down to the beach with it and hid it."

"Why?"

Her lovely, piquant face was bleak. "Because I was so terribly afraid Carla had killed him," she said simply.

"But you've changed your mind?"

"Yes. Carla doesn't act like a woman who has just murdered her husband. Oh, I know that must sound naive. I realize she could be outsmarting me. But Carla *is* my sister, I do *know* her.

"She hasn't been hiding anything this past week unless it's the quantity of her own drinking. I mean, she hasn't pretended to be broken-hearted about Greg; there has been no false grief. She's been surprisingly natural, except for calling you at four o'clock in the morning, but I think that was natural, too, under the circumstances.

"At first, though, I was afraid for her, and like an idiot, I suppose, I felt that I had to protect her. My only thought was to get rid of the bottle. I knew if I were to smash it the pieces might be found, and I couldn't trust the tide to take it out, so I hid it, temporarily, until I could find time to get rid of it for good."

He reached for his pipe and said, "Do you mind?" and she shook her head. But he didn't fill it, he just held it between his fingers, twirling the stem.

He asked, hating the question, "What made you think Greg Banning had been poisoned?"

She said, "I heard them talk about pumping out his stomach when we were at the hospital. If it had been a heart attack or a stroke they certainly wouldn't have been pumping out his stomach, so I thought of poison. Not *poison*, at first, I thought

of food poisoning, actually. Then I realized
everyone at the party had been eating the same
things and no one else had got sick.

"For that matter, I doubted if Greg had eaten
anything; I don't think he ever did at parties. So I
thought of drinks, and of course no one else ever
drank his brew, and he never offered it to them.

"The fact that he collapsed in the studio was
what made me suspicious of *that* Moses bottle,
rather than the one at the bar, and it would have
been easy for Carla to get to it anytime. All I
thought of, initially, was protecting Carla, which
I admit was stupid of me. But that's the way it
was."

Their eyes met. He said, "I don't think it was
stupid. I think it was understandable. But I'm
glad you told Higgins about it, and I'm glad you
told me."

Silence stretched between them, but it was a
warm silence. Finally she said, shakily, "The ice
in your coffee has melted," and he laughed.

"So has yours," he told her, and she laughed,
too, the shadows lifted from her blue eyes, the
tension gone between them, at least for the time
being.

22

CARLA CAME HOME in the middle of the afternoon, looking especially beautiful in a pale pink suit, but her face was flushed, her eyes a little too bright. She almost immediately suggested drinks, and when he and Clare declined she fixed herself a gin and tonic anyway.

He told her about Bertha Murphy, and was convinced that her shock was genuine.

"Poor woman!" she said. "But why would anyone set fire to her house, of all horrible things?"

"We don't know yet," he said.

"It would be the same as murder," Carla said, as Priscilla Standish had said earlier. "Who could possibly want to kill Bertha Murphy?"

He offered the thought quietly. "Perhaps the same person who killed Greg," he said.

Carla frowned. "I can't see why," she said. "I simply can't see why. Greg and Bertha Murphy had no connections."

Clare's voice was very clear. She said, each word distinct, "Perhaps Mrs. Murphy saw something she shouldn't have the night of the party."

"She wasn't even *here* when Greg died," Carla

protested. "She'd gone home, remember? I can't recall why."

"I think it was to change her shoes," Clare said.

"Her *shoes*?" Dr. Casey asked. "I thought she didn't hurt her ankle until just a couple of days ago."

"That's true," Clare agreed, "but her feet bothered her anyway, and she'd been on them quite a bit, setting everything up. I remember they were terribly swollen. She was awfully overweight—I suppose that might have had something to do with it."

Carla laughed shortly. "Ask the good doctor!" she suggested.

Clare ignored this. She said, "I remember Mrs. Murphy telling Bart Smith that her feet were killing her, and that she wanted to go get her old slippers. He told her she didn't need to come back, as Mary Blodgett was helping him and it was just a question of her keeping the platters on the dining-room table filled up with food and clearing off glasses. Mrs. Murphy wanted to come back though, swollen feet and all. Chances are that she needed the money, I suppose."

Casey turned to Carla. "Had she been working for you long?" he asked.

"Two or three summers," Carla said. "I'd already told her I'd like her to keep on, now that we were going to stay here year-round, and she seemed quite happy about that."

"How did you happen to find her?" Casey

asked, because good household help on the Cape
wasn't that easy to come by.

"Florence Page told me about her," Carla
said. "Greg had people coming from New York,
and I really needed someone. Florence told me
Mrs. Murphy was a sloppy-looking old thing, but
a very good worker—and she was, too. She always showed up, which is unusual on Cape Cod,
and she stayed as long as I needed her. Remember, the morning after Greg's death she insisted on coming back even though it was Labor
Day?"

He remembered. He remembered going out to
the kitchen and getting coffee, and Bertha Murphy had been there; a background person, someone who could be around without your really
being aware of her.

Carla got up, holding her empty glass. She said,
"Lon, come on, it's Sunday. Are you going to
make me drink alone?"

He fibbed. He said, "I'd like to join you but I
have an engagement, I have to leave."

"Fishing, I'll bet," she accused him.

He smiled. "Fishing," he said. Which, in one
sense at least, was the truth.

His "fishing expedition" took him to the
Blodgett's house, a small Cape Cod that was an
old one, he suspected—he still was no authority
on Cape Cod architecture—with low ceilings and
a quiet charm.

Mary and Percy were watching television in
the living room. Percy, huddled in his wheelchair, looked even more shrunken than he had

the last time Dr. Casey had seen him, but his welcome was genuinely cordial.

Mary, obviously, had been crying. Her eyes were red rimmed, and she said, before he could ask her, "I heard about Bertha on the radio." She shuddered. "What an awful way to die!"

"Had you seen her recently?"

"I went over to her place just yesterday morning, matter of fact," Mary said. "She phoned and asked if I was going uptown, she wanted a loaf of bread and a quart of milk. She'd sprained her ankle and she could barely get around the house, let alone drive her car."

Mary shook her head sadly. "She'd let herself go something terrible, Bertha had," she said. "All that weight! Didn't make it any easier with a sprained ankle. I thought about making a cake for her, but I figured it'd only add more pounds. I got the bread and milk for her and picked up some nice-looking apples and oranges they had in the market. We sat and talked awhile, and I told her to phone if she wanted anything. She had the phone right next to her chair in the living room."

"What time did you leave?" Dr. Casey asked.

"Toward noon. I got back in time to fix Percy's lunch."

"Did she have many friends, Mary?"

"Well, there was Pris Standish, of course; the three of us went to school together." Mary shook her head. "That was a long time ago. I don't know much about Bertha's other friends. She used to be active in the guild at the Catholic

church, but I don't think she'd done too much
lately."

"Did she have any relatives around here?"

"No. Only relative I know of that's still living is
her son out in California. Suppose he'll be flying
back for the service?"

"I don't know," Casey said.

Mary offered coffee, but he declined. He stood,
and Percy gave him a faint farewell smile.

Mary walked to the door with him, then, to his
surprise, followed him outside.

She said, "Doctor, I'm worried sick about
Percy. He hasn't got any interest in anything,
anymore. We used to play two-handed pinochle
together, but he's got no mind for it now. He said
the other day there wasn't much point to his living any longer. It scares me."

He patted her arm. He said, "I'll stop by during
the week and look him over."

"What Percy needs he's never going to get,"
Mary said. Her pale blue eyes seemed very far
away. "He needs Susan," she said. "I'd do anything in the world for him, but I can't bring her
back."

Susan. Mary, he realized, was talking about
their daughter.

He said, hesitantly, "Mary . . . ."

She managed the echo of a smile. "We'll get
by," she said.

He detoured, on his way home, to drive down
to the end of a road that overlooked the bay, but
this only made him wish that Clare was sitting in
the car beside him.

Once home, he checked with his answering service only to find that one of his patients was having severe abdominal pains.

He called promptly, decided that it sounded like appendicitis, called the town ambulance, and followed the ambulance to the hospital.

It was appendicitis, and after a surgeon had been located he went back home again just in time to get a call from the rescue squad asking him to suture an accident victim.

Even the Sunday after Labor Day, it seemed, could not be counted upon as a day of rest, and he began to think about what Clare had said. She was right. There were others around; it was about time, he thought whimsically, that he let them have some of the burden.

CLARE CALLED HIM Monday morning. He had just come back from making house calls, looked at himself in the mirror, and decided that a visit to the barbershop might be appropriate.

"Lon, are you very busy?" she asked, and his heart seemed to lurch when she spoke his name.

"No," he said. "Why?"

"Well, Carla's at the beauty parlor and then she's going out to lunch, and I wanted to talk to you. Last night Bob Fawcett called from New York—Greg's lawyer, remember?"

"Yes."

"He told Carla he thought it might be a good idea if we got all of Greg's paintings together and shipped them down there. Then if Carla decides to go back to the city with me she won't have to worry about someone breaking in here. Even if they didn't steal any of the paintings there's always the risk of vandalism.''

"That's true," he conceded.

"Actually," Clare said, "Carla didn't talk to Bob, I did. She wasn't up to it. She just kept on drinking after you left. She seemed terribly upset about Bertha Murphy. She got awfully maudlin about Bertha and Greg and life and everything else. I didn't quite know how to cope.''

He said grimly, "You should have called me.''

"I thought about it," she admitted, "but it's not fair to keep involving you.''

"I don't feel that way about it. I think you *know* I don't feel that way about it.''

"Well," she said, "anyway, I covered as best I could with Bob Fawcett, then this morning I spoke to Carla. She said to do whatever I thought right about Greg's paintings, but of course it isn't my decision.''

Dr. Casey said gently, "Just now, she may need you to make the decision for her.''

"Perhaps, but it's quite a responsibility. Greg *does* have a reputation and now that he's dead the value of his paintings will undoubtedly go up. Some of the earlier paintings really are wonderful, too. But—there's more to it than that, Lon.''

He caught a certain note in her voice and he said, alerted, "What is it, Clare?''

"I came out to the studio, after Carla left for the beauty parlor," she said. "I'm in here now. I decided to try to get everything together, first, to see just how much there is.''

"Yes?"

"Well. . .there are some paintings on the wall, I'm sure you know that, and some stashed around. Some are finished, some unfinished, some signed, some not signed. . .just what one might expect. But there's also a storage space, toward the back. It was locked, which I thought was rather odd, so I decided to try to find the key."

"Did you?"

"Yes. Greg didn't pick a very original hiding place, really. There were some keys under a pile of handkerchiefs in his top drawer and one did fit the storage closet door."

She paused, the silence grew longer, and finally he asked, "What's in the closet, Clare?"

"Paintings," she said, unhappily. "I'd rather not say any more about them. I wish you'd come out here and see them for yourself."

AT FIRST GLANCE, Gregory Banning's studio looked as if it had been transformed into an art exhibit. There were paintings propped everywhere.

Clare stood in the midst of them, wearing blue jeans and a faded smock, her copper hair tied back with a white ribbon. She looked like a teenager, unless you let your gaze linger on her face. Dr. Casey did, and saw again the tense expression that had become all too familiar. Her blue eyes were shadowed again and there was a tightness to her mouth he didn't like.

He indicated the paintings, trying to keep it
light. He said, "Greg was productive."

"Yes," said Clare, and added bitterly, "more
productive than we thought."

The paintings represented a surprising variety.
Casey had always thought of Gregory Banning
primarily as a portrait artist and there were portraits, to be sure, but there were also landscapes,
marines, even an abstract or two.

Clare, noting his surprise, said, "Greg experi-
mented, especially these past few years. He must
have realized he was slipping so he tried to alter
style. It works with some artists, I guess, but it
didn't with him. None of these are anything,
compared to his early work."

Casey said, puzzled, "Regardless of their quality, there's nothing wrong about any of them.
You sounded over the phone as if you'd found
something obscene."

A muscle in her jaw twitched. She said, "Well,
the paintings I mentioned are still in the storage
space. I'd rather bring them out one at a time,
just in case someone else wanders out here."

Her lovely face was rigid. She said stiffly,
"They're nudes."

Casey smiled. "Clare," he said, "come on,
now. Hasn't every artist done his share of nudes?
What's so—"

. Again, she interrupted him. She said, "It isn't
what they are—it's *who* they are and how they
were done. You'll see."

She seemed to square her shoulders as she
went to the back of the room and opened a low

door set into the far wall, so cleverly constructed that it was barely noticeable.

She said, tonelessly, "Okay. Prepare yourself."

She brought out a painting, back toward him, then turned it around.

"See what I mean?" she asked him.

23

THERE WERE FOURTEEN PAINTINGS in all, each more devastating in its way than the last.

Gregory Banning had indeed painted nudes, but he had done so with a touch peculiarly his own.

This was top-drawer pornographic art, done by a real genius. The skin tones were exquisite, contours beautiful, the technique perfect. There were touches reminiscent of the great masters, but all were done in a manner that was not only disgusting but evil and vicious.

Greg Banning had been *sick*. He had also left a legacy that might be described as fourteen invitations to murder.

The faces were absolutely recognizable, which was the filthiest part of all. Jane Bailey came first. He had painted her with her legs spread wide open, and an expression on her face that combined grossness and lust, defining them both.

He had painted Florence Page in the act of masturbating, while Tony Mayo lay in a coffin, his giant penis erect.

Brent Nickerson was handsome as a Greek god in his nudity, and he was also blatantly gay—

extravagantly made up, his mouth a scarlet slash
across his face as he fondled Hank Bailey, who lay
limply within the circle of his arms.

Carla was coupled with Robert Fawcett in the
midst of intercourse, and there were others, un-
known, one a blonde with chiseled features and
wide eyes. Doctor Casey wondered if she might
have been the paramour who once shared her
Chatham home with Gregory Banning.

The most haunting picture of all was the portrait of a young girl whose cloudlike dark hair and
ivory skin had been done with incredible mastery
She lay with her young breasts upthrust proudly,
doe eyes filled with anticipation, clearly eager for
sex even though there was a sense of very recent
virginity about her.

For whom was she ready? Greg? And who was
she?

Clare put the last of the paintings back into the
closet, closed the door, locked it.

She turned to Casey. She said simply, "Now you
see."

"Yes," he said.

"He was a fiend," she said. "I don't know what
to do about this. I don't know whether to tell Carla
or not. Maybe she already knows about them."

He said, "Thank God he didn't paint you."

"Yes." She met his eyes. "He had no reason to,
Lon."

"I realize that. Clare—these are all motive pro-
viders."

"I know," she said. "But he has distorted
everything so horribly."

"Even so," he pointed out, "any one of those portraits, held before a jury, could be damning evidence."

"Yes," Clare said, "I know that. Even Carla's."

He said, "Look, let's get out of here. Even the air seems fetid. Let's walk."

They went down the steps to the beach, walking across it toward the tide line where the sand was firm. At first she almost had to run to keep up with him, then, realizing this, he tailored his stride and they walked side by side.

The breeze blew tendrils of her hair into ringlets around her forehead, and she brushed them back. She said, "Dear God, everything is so beautiful, but he made it all so ugly."

Casey said slowly, "He was sick. I know that's become a cliché, but in this case it's true. He was very sick, even though he was a great artist."

Casey picked up a white beach pebble, worn smooth by the sand and the sea. He rubbed it between his fingers and he said, "The portraits make it clear, I'd say. Greg's murder was pure revenge. Someone must have planned it for a long time, someone who was willing to wait. They must have bought a Moses bottle somewhere, then waited their chance, filled it with methyl alcohol and *cassis* and substituted it the night of the party, either at the bar or in Greg's studio."

"The bottle I hid," Clare said, "did it have poison in it?"

"No, but neither did the one that had been on the bar. Not that is, if it's the same one we found back in its place in the dining-room cupboard. We think there's a third Moses bottle, still missing.

Either the murderer managed to take it away that night or to hide it some place where he could get it later.''

"Well, they've all been back," Clare said.

"What do you mean?"

"Tony was around, of course, and the Baileys, Florence Page, even Brent Nickerson. All came back within the next day or so to see Carla and offer their condolences. A number of others who had been at the party stopped by, too. It would have been simple enough for any of them to have retrieved the Moses bottle; there was so much going on, people coming and going.''

"Possibly," he said. "Clare...."

"Yes?"

"The police should see those paintings. At least Bert Higgins should. I suppose Lieutenant Brigham, he's state police with the D.A.'s office, should see them, too, but maybe we can stop with Higgins.''

"I hope so," she said. "Those paintings could ruin a lot of people, most of them innocent. At least I imagine there is only one guilty person, don't you?"

"Yes," he nodded. "Yes, in this case, I imagine so.''

"It seems wrong to crucify all of them," she said.

"I can't make promises," he said, "because if I did I might not be able to keep them. But I'll do my best.''

She reached out and found his hand, and clasped her fingers through his.

He said, "You're cold.''

She said, "No, not really."

But still he put his arm around her and drew her close, and they walked like that, without saying anything, for quite a long time.

DR. CASEY WAS PREOCCUPIED during office hours that afternoon, thankful that there were no cases that required his total concentration.

After he had closed and locked his office door he sat for a long time at his desk, literally lost in thought, then he dialed Eleanor Chase's number.

He came directly to the point with her. "Eleanor," he asked, "do a lot of people go to that Community Exchange in Orleans?"

"Indeed they do," Eleanor assured him. "It's one of the few places left where you can sometimes get a sleeper."

"A sleeper?"

"The things one finds in grandmother's attic can be either treasure or trash," Eleanor said. "Sometimes people who don't know too much about old things can't differentiate. That, Lon, is why I want to be sure you don't part with any of your things until I go over them for you."

"So, then," he said, "a sleeper is something with value and a low price?"

"Exactly."

"Who runs the Exchange, would you know?"

"Betty Dodge, presently," said Eleanor. "Why?"

"I wanted to ask her something," he said vaguely, and rang off before Eleanor could ask him what that something was.

Mrs. Dodge became friendly immediately when he told her he was a friend of Eleanor Chase's, but the Exchange had processed thousands of items over the season, she explained.

They kept records, of course, but to unearth a single item would rival searching a haystack for the proverbial needle. Still, if it were really important to him she would somehow make time to look through the books.

He told her that it might be tremendously important, and that he would be eternally grateful for anything she could do for him. Dr. Casey had a way with him at such moments, and Mrs. Dodge promised to get back to him.

Next he called the police station. Bert Higgins answered the phone gruffly.

"Where have you been?" he demanded.

"Working. I do have a practice, remember."

"How can I forget? Look, Brigham's got his troopers crawling all over the Murphy cottage. He seems to think I've missed the boat."

"Doesn't he always?"

"Well, maybe he's got a case this time," the chief admitted. "It's over a week since Banning died, and where are we? There's still too much missing."

"Perhaps not." Casey hesitated. "There's a painting out in Banning's studio, Bert," he said. "I want you to take a look at it."

He phoned Clare and said, "I just want to show him that one picture. There's no need to produce the others now and maybe there never will be."

Clare said, "I hope not. Who was she, Lon?"

"I'm not sure," he admitted. "But I think Higgins will be."

There was one more phone call to make. He dialed Olson's Package Store and asked for Frank Olson, and was told that Frank Olson had gone to Hyannis on business.

Mary Blodgett wasn't there, either. "She was supposed to come in, but she called and said her husband's in kind of a bad way and she felt she ought to stay with him. This is Pete Henderson, doc. Can I help you?" Dr. Casey was asked. And the possibility arose that it was quite possible Pete Henderson *could* help him.

Pete Henderson had worked all day the previous Saturday. He also had a surprisingly good memory.

DR. CASEY AND CHIEF HIGGINS drove across to The Heights in the yellow station wagon. The Banning's driveway was empty; Carla, then, had not yet returned.

Clare was waiting for them in the studio. She produced the portrait and the chief pursed his lips as he looked at it.

"Yes," he said, "I know who she is. *Was*, I guess I should say. It's Susan Blodgett."

24

"SHE WAS LOVELY," Clare said softly.

"Yes," said the chief, "she was."

"You never did find out who the man was who'd been with her the night she died, did you?" Casey asked.

"No," the chief said. "We talked to her friends, kids her own age, they all knew that Susan had an older man. Someone rich and famous, a couple of them told me. So if it was Banning, that fits right in."

He sighed. "Susan was waitressing at the Clam Shack that summer," he said. "She ran into a lot of people there. She wasn't a bad kid, but she was probably—looking for a good time. Mary and Percy had been married a long time when they had her. They doted on her, but from what I hear they were awfully strict with her.

"She was a smart kid, though, and it wasn't too hard for her to dupe them. She got in with a bad crowd, drugs, the whole bit, but she was smart enough to never be around when we staged a raid. Somehow she always slipped by us. If she did get involved with Banning, she was no ingenue. Even so, he must have been way out of her league."

"I would say so," Dr. Casey agreed dryly.

"Mrs. Evans," the chief said almost apologetically, "I'll have to take this picture with me."

"Yes, I realize that," Clare told him.

The phone rang, startling all three of them. Clare picked up the receiver and said, puzzled, "Why, yes, of course I will." Then, "Carla, where *are* you?"

Casey saw her eyes widen. She said, incredulously, "I don't believe it! Yes. All right!"

She hung up, and it was Dr. Casey she turned to. She said flatly, "She's eloped."

"*Eloped*? With whom, for God's sake?"

"Frank Olson," said Clare. "The man who runs the liquor store—"

"Your sister and Olson?" It was Bert Higgins's turn to be incredulous. "It doesn't make sense," he said.

Clare said, "She called collect from Boston. Logan Airport. They're flying somewhere, she wouldn't say where. She says they're going to get married as soon as they can, then she'll let me know where I can reach them. She says they *will* be coming back. She wanted you to know that, Chief."

"Decent of her," the chief said wryly.

"I didn't realize she even knew Olson," Casey said.

"Oh, yes," Clare said. "Sometimes he used to deliver liquor to her himself, and he came over to see her last week after Greg died. She said afterward that he was an awfully nice person."

Clare smiled, a tired little smile. She said, "Maybe they deserve each other. Maybe they'll both swear off and go to A.A. and join a lecture circuit. But meantime—" her smile faded "—it's just one more thing."

One more thing...of many, many things. Dr. Casey wanted to take her in his arms and comfort her, and would have if Bert Higgins had not been present.

She said, "What comes now, Chief Higgins? I'm not like my sister about alcohol, but do you think we could go back in the house and have a drink?"

He did, so they sat in the living room looking out over an ocean touched with twilight's amethyst now, the surf low, lapping the shore.

Dr. Casey found his pipe and this time he did fill and light it.

The chief, watching him gloomily, said, "We could be wrong, you know." And, when Casey merely looked across at him levelly, "All right, then. Did you suspect Mary from the beginning?"

Casey shook his head. "No," he said. "As a matter of fact, I thought at first it was probably Carla, but that's probably because so often it is either the husband or the wife. Later, I was very much afraid that it was Clare."

He avoided meeting her eyes. "That, I admit, was an emotional reaction on my part," he said. "When I started thinking things out I logically realized that this was a definite case of 'murder with malice aforethought.' A clear case of revenge, but I never thought of Mary Blodgett in connection with it."

Clare said, "Lon, are you and the chief *sure*?"

"Just about," he told her.

"You see, Mary is one of those background people, much as Bertha Murphy was in her way. You don't really notice her in a crowd. I got to thinking about that. She was on hand the night of the party, she went home and got her husband's supper, but she came back to help out later. Much of the time she was going back and forth to the bar and keeping the stock refilled, and she was also keeping an eye on the buffet in the dining room. She was the one person who could have carried a Moses bottle out to the kitchen and refilled it without anyone thinking anything about it, and I think that is precisely what she did."

"You think she brought the bottle with the poison in it when she came back here after dinner?" the chief asked.

"No, I think she brought it with her when she came here in the first place. She always carries a tote bag around with her that looks like it was made out of a piece of carpeting. She calls it her McGillicuddy and usually she has some knitting in it, and God knows what else.

"My guess is that she brought the poison over here with her in her own Moses bottle, helped Barton Smith set up the bar, and put her bottle right out on it. Smith kept the bottle down under somewhere, anyway. It was reserved for Greg Banning's own use.

"I think Mary's only mistake was that she thought it would take longer for the methyl alcohol to kill Banning than it did. And I think I know the reason for that, too.''

"I think I have a guess of my own,'' Bert Higgins admitted. "Percy Blodgett worked in a hardware store for years, and back in those days, you could get methyl alcohol to use as a varnish remover. There weren't the restrictions there are now. My guess is that Mary has had a bottle of it for years, and I seem to remember your telling me that the older the stuff gets the more potent it is.''

"Exactly,'' Casey agreed. "Actually, I don't imagine that Mary was too concerned about when her poison would take effect, she just had to be sure to get her Moses bottle back. So she went home and made Percy's supper as she always did, taking *Greg Banning*'s Moses bottle, filled with gin and *cassis*, with her, and brought it back again later. After that, she had to make one more substitution. She had to put the bottle with the poison in it back in her McGillicuddy, and she figured she'd be home clear. Susan and Percy would both be avenged, in her mind, and I'm sure that was all that mattered to her.''

He paused. "She just might have got away with it except for one thing,'' he said.

"What?'' Clare asked him.

"Bertha Murphy.''

"Do you think Bertha saw the Moses bottle in Mary's tote bag?''

"Not necessarily, though she may have. I do think, though, that she knew Mary had such a bottle.''

"When we came back the next day to get the bottle, Bertha was working here," the chief said. "I asked her if she knew where the Moses bottle was, and she showed me. It wouldn't have been too hard for her to put two and two together. . . ."

"Exactly. Even to say something to Mary like, 'You have a bottle like that, don't you?'

"Bertha had been around a long time, remember. Obviously Mary knew Gregory Banning was the man who indirectly caused her daughter's death, maybe Bertha did, too. So maybe the more Mary thought about Bertha, the greater her fear became.

"Then Bertha sprained her ankle, and it became a golden opportunity in Mary's mind. She went out to see her, but it wasn't on Saturday morning, as she told us. It was Saturday night and with the fruit and the bread and the milk she took Bertha a bottle of muscatel wine. Bertha liked anything sweet.

"Mary went into the liquor store and bought the muscatel Saturday evening, because Pete Henderson remembers it. He wanted to go get a grinder to bring back for his supper and Mary minded the store for him for a few minutes."

Bert Higgins said thoughtfully, "You know that heep she drives around has a four-wheel drive."

"I hadn't really noticed," Casey said.

"I have. Also Mary would know the trails through those woods like the palm of her hand, too. She's lived around here all her life."

"Exactly." Casey was thoughtful. Then he said, "I think we'll find that maybe Mary did pay Bertha a visit in the morning after all, and that something Bertha said, probably about the Moses bottle, maybe settled her mind for her, so she went back later with the bottle of muscatel. That must have been when she set the fire, but she didn't light it. That came later. She just got things ready. Rags, kerosene. All she needed to do later was to strike the match."

"I'd also guess," said the chief, "that she cut the phone wires on that evening visit. Don't know if I mentioned it, but they *were* cut, which left Bertha Murphy pretty helpless. She wouldn't have got far on that ankle."

Clare shuddered. She said, "It's fiendish."

"When someone plots to kill it usually is," Casey said quietly.

The chief said, "I know Eleanor Chase said those Moses bottles aren't rare, but I've stopped in myself at a few places to see if I could find one and I don't think they're all that easy to come by anymore. Do you suppose Mary's was an old family heirloom?"

"I doubt it," Casey said. "I think I know where she got it, but we'll get back to that later. I'm more interested in finding out what she did with it."

"If we're right about all this, she smashed it," Chief Higgins said. "We found pieces of green glass in the shed back of Bertha's cottage. I imagine Mary figured the shed would burn up, too."

THEY WRAPPED Susan Blodgett's portrait in an old sheet and put it in the back of the station wagon. At Dr. Casey's house, Higgins transferred the portrait to the police cruiser.

He said, "I'm going to have to show this to Brigham, and I don't want to."

"I don't blame you," Casey said.

"Look, I've got to think about this a little more before I do anything," the chief decided. "I could use a bit to eat. How about going over to Jessie's with me?"

"Okay. But let me check the answering service first."

There were four messages for him, two of which could wait, the third was in answer to his earlier call to Betty Dodge. The Community Exchange ledger had shown that a Moses bottle had been sold in early August. One of the women working at the sales desk that day had remembered the purchaser, because she did some sewing for her from time to time.

"A little woman named Mary Blodgett," Mrs. Dodge reported.

The fourth message was a final irony. Mary Blodgett herself had called to say that Percy was not at all well and she wished Dr. Casey would come to the house.

He went and Bert Higgins went with him, and dinner at Jessie's Kitchen was forgotten.

25

MARY BLODGETT SAT on a couch in the hospital waiting room, the same couch, Dr. Casey realized, that Carla and Clare had been sitting on little more than a week ago.

He took her into the meditation room, just as he had taken them, and said, "We've got Percy in Intensive Care, Mary. He's had another stroke, and he's still unconscious. There's no point in your seeing him tonight."

She looked up at him, and she asked bluntly, "Will there be a tomorrow?"

"I don't know," he admitted.

She was holding a handkerchief between her fingers and she twisted it again and again. She said, "It's no use, doctor. I know Percy's going to die. There's no reason for him to live."

She looked ancient, totally spent, yet she said, almost belligerently, "I only did what I had to do. Percy shouldn't have blamed me!"

"What did he blame you for, Mary?" he asked softly.

She looked up at him swiftly, then shook her head and, despite himself, he felt pity for her. He took a chance. He said, "Mary, we know," then he blanched inwardly at his own lack of professionalism, imagining what Bert Higgins would have to say about this.

She was still stubborn, but she avoided his eyes, "What do you know about?"

"We know you bought a Moses bottle in the Community Exchange in Orleans. We know you had some methyl alcohol Percy brought home from the hardware store a long time ago. When Bart Smith asked you to help him out at the Bannings' party you realized this was your chance to get even with Greg Banning."

He asked cautiously, "How did you find out about Susan and Greg Banning?"

Her tired eyes blazed briefly, then the light seemed to drain from them. She said, "I saw that picture he painted. I was cleaning up one day, out in his studio. He was out walking the beach. Usually I didn't go into the studio much, but he was expecting some visitors and Mrs. Banning said to me, 'Mary, you'd better go straighten up, just don't move any of his things around too much.' So I did just that, but I spilled a bottle of turpentine. I went to look for some rags to wipe it up, and that's how I happened on his closet. I found out later, when I went back to get the picture, that he kept it locked most of the time, but it was open then.

"I saw he had pictures stacked away in there, and I was curious," she said this defensively. "Everyone was always saying he was such a great artist so I thought I'd look, and my God, I couldn't believe it. Then, all of a sudden, there was Susan, and. . .I knew.

"It all fitted in. That summer. Susan working. Banning here. I knew it was someone older, a summer person, someone rich. I even had an idea what he looked like. A friend of mine saw Susan with him once at a bar up Cape, only it was dim, she didn't get too clear a look, just enough to give me an impression. Without that picture, I might never have put it together. With the picture . . ."

She said, "I don't know why I didn't slash it to pieces or set fire to it then and there. I guess I was numb."

"I imagine you must have been."

"Anyway, there wasn't time. I put the pictures back and sopped up the turpentine as best I could and got out of there. Then, right after Labor Day, the Bannings went back to New York, but I planned one day I'd get even with him, for Percy's sake."

"So you waited, and the right time finally came."

"Yes," said Mary. "It would have been all right, too, except for Bertha."

"The afternoon when the chief came to get the Moses bottle out of the Banning house, it set Bertha to thinking. When I stopped to see her Saturday morning, she asked me about my Moses bottle. She knew I had one like it. She'd seen it at my house. I'd told her I'd given it to my niece in Connecticut for a birthday present, but she got a funny look on her face; I don't think she believed me, and I couldn't take the chance. So I took her a bottle of muscatel that night, brought her the evening paper, too, saw to it that she was settled comfortably.''

Mary sighed. ''I told her I'd got a flat coming over, so not to mind if she heard a little noise outside, I'd be changing the tire. I had the kerosene and the rags in the car and I got everything all ready. Then I cut the phone wires and went back home and watched TV with Percy. It was a lot later when I went back there. . . .''

Mary shut her eyes tightly. She said, ''I don't want to think about it.''

''Once it was over, did you go back home?'' Casey asked her.

''Yes, that was the bad part. I'd got kerosene all over my wool gloves, so I put them in the kitchen sink. Next morning Percy wheeled himself out to the kitchen to make himself a cup of coffee, like he sometimes did, and he smelled the gloves. He asked me where the kerosene came from and like a fool I told him I'd been fixing Bertha's stove for her the day before.

''He didn't think any more about it till this afternoon, when the paper came. There was a story in it about the fire. It said Bertha's cottage had been heated by electric heaters, but the fire was started with kerosene, and that they thought it was arson.

''Percy read the story and he looked right at me. Somehow he *knew*. I won't ever forget the look in his eyes.''

Someone coughed. Dr. Casey looked up to see Bert Higgins standing in the doorway.

"Mary, the chief said, "they say maybe you should come see Percy, for just a minute."

His eyes met Casey's, and he nodded ever so slightly. He said, "No need for you to hang around here any longer, Pete."

Dr. Casey could not have agreed more.

He walked back through the hospital lobby, and out the wide glass doors into the clear, September night. There was a sickle moon and polished stars; there should, somewhere, also be some kind of promise, some kind of hope.

He and the chief had driven Mary to the Hyannis hospital in the police cruiser; this now gave him the option of waiting until Bert Higgins was free—which might be a while—or of getting some other form of transportation back to Devon.

Even as he was thinking this he saw, disbelievingly, that his own yellow station wagon was parked almost in front of the entrance, and the girl in the driver's seat got out and walked toward him.

He could see her face clearly in the light of an arc lamp, and she looked anxious. She said, "Lon, I hope you don't mind. The chief said he was apt to get involved, and you might like to have your own car. He said he thought you'd appreciate it if I drove it over."

He grinned at this attempt on Higgins's part to play Cupid, and was briefly surprised at the intensity of his own sudden sense of joy.

He stood, looking down at her, and there were so many things he wanted to say to her that he was momentarily unable to say anything at all.

She still looked anxious, and so he began to speak, almost desperate to find the right words.

"Clare . . ." he said.

"Yes?"

"You mentioned once that Carla had spoken to you about me."

Her lips twisted in a smile. She said, "Carla spoke about you quite frequently."

"Well, this particular time she told you that she thought there would always be a shadow between me and anyone . . . anyone who might consider caring for me," he went on, finding the going on this very rough.

"Yes," Clare said. "Yes, she did say that."

He swallowed hard. He said, "I think you should know that she was wrong." His voice was unsteady. He said, "There *is* no shadow, my dearest," and he saw tears shimmer, suddenly, in her eyes. "There is no shadow at all."

Be a detective.
See if you can solve the...

Raven House
MINUTE
MYSTERY

On the following page is Raven House
MINUTE MYSTERY #1, "A Lie Gets the Ax."

Every month each Raven House book will feature a
MINUTE MYSTERY, a unique little puzzler designed
to let *you* do the sleuthing!

Check your answer by calling (in U.S.A. only)
1-800-528-1404 during the months of August,
September and October 1981. Canadian and U.S.
residents may obtain the solution by writing any time
during or after this period to:

Raven House MINUTE MYSTERY
1440 South Priest Drive
Tempe, AZ 84281
U.S.A.

A LIE GETS THE AX

"The body's under the woodpile, but remember—you gotta keep me outa this," whined Stig Carona, casting shifty eyes at Professor Fordney and Inspector Kelley. Sniffing through a nose that an ungenerous nature had placed at an unlovely angle and licking lips cut on the bias, Stig twisted his greasy cap in nervous fingers.

An hour later the three men got out of a police car and walked to a clump of bushes in Wilson's woods.

"Bill and Jake were fightin' in front of that shack over there," Stig explained, pointing to a clearing. "Jake knocked Bill down, then grabbed an ax. When Bill got up Jake hit him over the head with it a couple of times. Then he dragged the body toward the shack. He must've thought he heard somethin' 'cause he propped it up against the house and walked over this way. I knew if he found me here I'd get what Bill got, so I lammed to the road, jumped in my car and went for the cops."

Fordney observed bloodstains on the shack about three feet from the ground, which appeared to bear out Stig's story. Some freshly cut firewood spattered with dark stains lay near a chopping block.

Opening the door of the shack the professor was about to enter when Kelley called from the yard. "The body's under the woodpile, all right. Gad, what a sight!"

But Fordney's interest at the moment was not the body but a bright, clean, shining ax standing in the far corner of the shack's single room. Carrying it by its battered handle, he took it outside. At the professor's quiet words Stig turned with a startled look.

"Unless," said Fordney, "you want to be placed under arrest for murder immediately, you will tell us the truth about this crime."

How did Fordney know Stig's account was untrue?

From **Minute Mysteries** by Austin Ripley
Copyright © 1949 by Opera Mundi, Paris.